KIT CARSON'S WAY

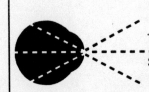

This Large Print Book carries the
Seal of Approval of N.A.V.H.

KIT CARSON'S WAY

TOM CURRY

WHEELER PUBLISHING
A part of Gale, Cengage Learning

Detroit • New York • San Francisco • New Haven, Conn • Waterville, Maine • London

GALE
CENGAGE Learning

LIBRARY OF CONGRESS CATALOGING-IN-PUBLICATION DATA

Curry, Tom, 1900–
    Kit Carson's way / by Tom Curry. — Large print ed.
        p. cm. — (Wheeler Publishing large print western) (A Rio
    Kid western series)
    ISBN-13: 978-1-4104-3983-3 (pbk.)
    ISBN-10: 1-4104-3983-6 (pbk.)
    1. Large type books. I. Title.
PS3505.U9725K58 2011
813'.52—dc22   2011017531

Published in 2011 by arrangement with Golden West Literary Agency.

Printed in the United States of America
1 2 3 4 5   15 14 13 12 11

ED206

KIT CARSON'S WAY

CHAPTER I
OLD AND NEW

Bigfoot Wallace thought it amusing, but the Rio Kid's face was inscrutable as they watched the baiting of the young man in ragged gray.

"He's gettin' on his hoss shore enough, Rio Kid," chortled "Bigfoot," his huge body slouched in the shade.

In this year of 1867 the Civil War was still fresh in the minds of men. But here, the Rio Kid thought, was a sample of the rancor still existing that was not to his liking. After all, this young fellow in gray had been a soldier, and probably had fought as valiantly for what he had considered right as Bob Pryor, the Rio Kid, had fought himself — though on the opposite side.

And in Pryor's mind there was no reason for these men of New Mexico to act as they were acting now, though New Mexico had gone with the Union. Bob Pryor had been with the Union Army also, and his native state was Texas.

More formally, he was Captain Robert Pryor who, through the four awful years of the War Between the States had fought under Sheridan, Custer and Grant. War's horrors had left a certain grimness about him, as was inevitable, but his eyes were still boyish, with a deep blue glint that showed his devil-may-care fighting courage.

Watching the scene before him now, he was a fine figure of a man, every inch a soldier, though a frown creased his broad forehead. His face was clean-shaven and bronzed, and, reminiscent of the recent days when he had been a soldier, he wore his blue tunic, and his trousers with the broad yellow cavalry stripe down each leg were tucked into high black Army boots with silver spurs. The rowels, however, were not as large as those usually affected in the West.

His Stetson was cocked at a rakish angle, showing his closely cropped, crisp chestnut hair. Broad of shoulder, and narrow-waisted, his was the ideal weight and height for a cavalryman.

Strapped about his waist was a three-inch-wide black sword belt. Slung across his chest were cartridge belts with pleated holsters in which were his .45 Colt revolvers, and two more pistols were hidden in shoulder holsters under his shirt. Nor were they weapons merely for display, for four years in the Army, and earlier scout training on the Rio Grande had made him a dead shot.

He had scouted for Custer, had been the famous fighter's aide for a time. Naturally, with such years of fighting behind him, Bob Pryor was already a veteran, young as he was.

One other thing his Army training had given him, that would endure throughout his life — his passion for neatness and orderliness. It showed in the way he kept his clothing — always spick and span — in the way his saddle and bridle gleamed, and in the tiptop condition of his dun mount, Saber, his constant companion.

Saber was not far away now, one of three horses held by another constant companion of the Rio Kid — Celestino Mireles. A slim Mexican youth who had attached himself to the Rio Kid when Bob Pryor had saved his life in a Mexican bandit raid, young Mireles was sure to be found wherever the Rio Kid rode in his wanderings throughout the wide West.

Mireles was a tall youth whose skin was the rich dark creaminess of the Spanish dons who were his forebears, whose nose was the curved one of an eagle's beak, and whose eyes were inky black and deep-set. Right now the eyes were half closed, for he was drowsing on his feet as he held the three horses — his own pinto, the Rio Kid's mousy dun, and Bigfoot Wallace's oversized black.

War veteran though Saber was, also, and the fastest thing on legs the Rio Kid had ever met, he was not exactly a prepossessing mount. Though men wise to horseflesh would quickly guess his courage and stamina. And they would know, from the black stripe that ran down his back, that he was of "the breed that never dies."

Even as the lack of beauty of the Rio Kid's mount was self-evident, so was his bad temper — with all save the Rio Kid — for Saber was always spoiling for a fight. He was now. His mirled eye was rolling wickedly as he measured the distance to Bigfoot Wallace's black, with the plain intention of biting a chunk from the hide of the other horse, if possible.

That, apparently was Saber's idea of relaxation while the Rio Kid rested after a pause in this little New Mexican town with his trail mate, Mireles, and Bigfoot Wallace.

Wallace, who drove the mail from Texas to

Santa Fe, had ridden north with the Rio Kid for a short hunting trip after elk in the Sangre de Cristo Mountains. Bigfoot had not earned his nickname because of the size of his pedal extremities, for everything about him was big.

He had come by the appellation, in fact, in a way that had nothing to do with his own size. For the search he had been making for years for a Lipan Indian whose moccasin track was fourteen inches long had long ago caused him to be dubbed "Bigfoot," and the name stuck.

Wallace stood six-feet-four, weighed two hundred and forty, and his close-cut beard was sprinkled with gray. However, though he was fifty, he was as powerful in body and spirit as he had been as a young man. An Indian fighter, scout and soldier, Bigfoot Wallace was a man to ride the river with.

His wide mouth was spread in a grin now, as he listened to the altercation over near the porch of the store that overlooked the dusty plaza.

"Now look here, Johnny Reb," a loud-mouthed man over there was shouting angrily, "we don't want none of yore lip!" He added some epithets which drew snickers from the crowd. "What's yore handle?"

"I told you, suh," the young man in the

11

tattered gray uniform replied in a soft drawl. "It's Barron — Lieutenant Arthur Barron, C.S.A., it was until the War ended. I rode under Stonewall Jackson till his untimely death."

"He looks mighty hungry," thought the Rio Kid, edging closer.

The young fellow in tattered gray who called himself Barron was around six feet tall. His hair was black, his dark eyes deep-sunken, and his well-chiseled nose showed good breeding. He was extremely gaunt, though, and his lips were parched. The Rio Kid, a sharp observer, decided he must be faint from hunger. The horse he rode was a fine gray, long of limb and with curving neck and well-combed mane. Grazing at the coarse grass in the plaza were a dozen more animals he had in charge, as fine a bunch as the Rio Kid had ever seen. They showed their Kentucky strain, so superior in speed and appearance, though not always in stamina, to the chunky Western mustang.

"We don't go for traitors in New Mexico," announced the thick-set fellow on the porch, his arms belligerently akimbo. "You take the out-trail pronto and don't stop till we can't see yore dust, savvy?"

"I thought the War was over," muttered Barron wearily. "At least, out this way. Back in Kentucky —"

"Shut up. We don't want yore kind of skunk here, I tell yuh!"

The Rio Kid liked the man on the porch less and less. He wore fine boots, and black trousers, with a pearl-handled .45 showing in the belt, and a white shirt with sleeves rolled up, and a black string tie. He was bare-headed and had evidently just stepped from the store which apparently was his. He had a thick-lipped, sullen mouth, small, beady eyes, and a flat nose over a sandy mustache. His hair was a washed-out, dead shade.

The building before which he stood was divided into two parts. The sign on the right said:

JED HANNIGAN
GROCERIES AND SUPPLIES

The one on the left read:

WEEKLY GAZETTE
JED HANNIGAN, EDITOR

"Hey, Hannigan!" a man called from the small crowd. "Ask him what Jeff Davis has for breakfast!"

"I'll be ridin'," Barron said with dignity,

swinging to his gray horse.

"Halt!" Hannigan ordered, an idea coming into his head. "As mayor of this town, I demand yuh pay the toll charge for the grass them cayuses of yores have et, Johnny Reb. It'll be twenty dollars."

More snickers went up at this.

"I have no money," replied Barron simply, "and I don't believe what you say, suh."

The man who had yelled out the jest about Jeff Davis suddenly seized Barron's arm as he was about to mount, and jerked him so hard that Barron, off balance, fell, landing heavily on his back in the dust. A roar of mirth went up.

The fellow who had laid hands on Barron was a huge man, with a round, moon face, a permanently open mouth with hanging lower lip and cowlike brown eyes. He wore chaps and riding boots with big spurs, and a great Stetson with its chin-strap dangling loose. Leather cuffs covered his thick wrists, but not his hamlike hands.

"Hold him, Stensen!" someone shouted.

Barron leaped to his feet, his temper snapped. His bony fist whizzed with terrific speed straight to Stensen's surprised face, connecting with the man's thick nose. It spurted blood.

Stensen howled with pain and stunned

rage, staggered by the unexpected force of the blow.

Hannigan yanked his pistol from holster, but just as he raised it the Rio Kid jumped into the fray.

His Army Colt banged. Hannigan dropped his gun as though it had suddenly become red-hot. He blinked, the nearness of Pryor's slug taking away his breath and nerve.

For an instant there was silence, as the echoes of Pryor's shot rolled across the plaza to the painted mountains beyond. Then a dozen armed men started for Barron and the Rio Kid. Citizens who had just been watching the sport of baiting a Johnny Reb, turned and ducked for cover.

"Wait!" bellowed the Rio Kid, Colt in hand.

With that Army officer's voice of his which had enabled him to make himself heard over the roar of battle, as well as his commanding way, he made this bunch promptly obey, unconsciously awed by his leashed strength.

"I knew Abe Lincoln, boys," he shouted, "and he wouldn't have liked this sort of thing, not even now, with him murdered. The War *is* over. Let this stranger go."

It was a close call. Ole Stensen was cursing, holding his bloody nose. On the porch, Jed Hannigan had collected his wits after the frightening bullet had shaken him.

"String 'em both up!" he shouted angrily, shaking his fist at the Rio Kid.

As though used to obeying Hannigan's orders, several of the ringleaders stepped toward Barron and Pryor. Bigfoot Wallace eased over to stand by his friend, and Mireles unshipped the carbine from under Saber's stirrup strap.

A moment later they were at it, fists and boots flying. Barron, the Rio Kid and Bigfoot, took the initiative and sailed into the bunched gang. Unwilling to kill anybody if it was not necessary, the Rio Kid decided to chasten them with blows.

He finished Barron's work by dropping the big Stensen with a skillful punch to the point of the jaw. Bigfoot Wallace, a grin on his bearded lips, picked up bodily a dark-faced man in the van and hurled him at his friends.

Barron lashed out at two who were reaching to pull him down.

Within a minute they had halved the enemy. Cursing, fallen men crouched in the dust, dazed by the punches of hard, trained fists.

"No, no!" cried Mireles. "No, no, senor! Hold zat!"

Carbine up, he was covering Hannigan,

who, eyes flashing, again sought to start shooting.

The opposition suddenly quit. They did not like the power of the Rio Kid and the mighty Bigfoot Wallace's utter disregard of odds in a rough-and-tumble. The trio stood there, ready for more, but nobody else came at them.

"Go on, pick up yore hosses and ride, Barron," the Rio Kid ordered. "We'll give yuh a start."

"Thanks," Barron murmured, but the single word and his grateful glance spoke volumes.

He mounted his gray and rode over to move his Kentucky horses out of town. Mireles, his carbine ready, was watching Hannigan every second. But no further attempt to stop Barron or to fight Pryor and his partners was made.

"You'll pay for this," bawled Hannigan, smarting at the humiliation. He shook his fist at the Rio Kid.

"Any time yuh want to collect, Mister," Pryor drawled contemptuously.

The sharp-eyed Rio Kid saw to it that no guns were pulled. When Barron had pushed his horses off toward the gap to the north of the settlement, Pryor and Bigfoot Wallace backed to their own horses. The trio mounted and rode around the *Gazette* office and the central plaza.

Bigfoot Wallace chuckled as he glanced back over his brawny shoulder.

"A man who travels with you, Rio Kid," he observed cheerfully, "can always be shore of a first-class riot sooner of later. If I wasn't runnin' the mail for Uncle Sam I'd stick to yuh like a leech!"

"Johnny Reb or not," grunted the Rio Kid, "they were wrong, Bigfoot. A man has the right to a new chance in life."

"True enough." Wallace nodded, taking a chunk of black Navy-cut tobacco from his buckskin-coat pocket and biting off a chew. "I didn't think when I laughed at that feller Barron. Wonder where he'll head for?"

The Rio Kid and his companions had no trouble leaving the town. The men they had tangled with sent catcalls after them but no shots, for the distance was too great to hope for a hit when the three cut over and hit the north trail, riding in the hanging dust from Barron's bunch of horses.

CHAPTER II
TROUBLE

As they climbed to the heights over the town, the Rio Kid drew in deep breaths of the crisp, tangy air. Piñons and cedars grew on the slopes and the painted rocks were gorgeous. In the clear air, as he looked down on the valley he could see for fifty miles.

"This New Mexico Territory is mighty pretty country, boys," he remarked soberly.

"Nothin' handsomer," agreed Bigfoot Wallace, a leathery cheek pushed out by his cud.

They overtook Art Barron, the ex-Confederate soldier, a few miles outside Hannigan's settlement. He looked around, and when he saw who it was he pulled back to speak to the Rio Kid.

"I didn't have a chance to thank you right, suh. It was mighty white of yuh. You fought on the other side?"

"Yes. Under Custer most of the time. But the War's over, and my home's Texas."

Close to the young Southerner as he was now, the Rio Kid could see that Barron's face was more peaked than he at first noticed.

"What say we draw into that gully and have a bite?" the Rio Kid suggested. "Join us, Barron? We shot a buck yesterday and Bigfoot's the best cook this side of N'Orleans."

Barron accepted with alacrity, but sought to conceal the fact that he was practically out of provisions. Mireles gathered piñon sticks and soon had a hot bed of coals for the broiling of steaks. With hardtack from their saddle-bags, and coffee made with water from a clear mountain rill, they feasted.

It was easy enough to draw Barron out, for the Rio Kid was skillful at such work. Without seeming to be inquisitive, he learned that Barron, who was about his own age, had returned home from the War to discover that his father's plantation had been seized for debt. His father had been killed in the first year of the holocaust and his mother had died soon after.

His two sisters had been married, and had gone away. Young Barron had taken what little cash he could obtain, the best of his horses, and had started West. He was grateful that he still had the animals, which had been raised by the Negroes on the Barron place and carefully concealed from raiders. For if there was one thing the young Southerner loved more than another, it was horses. He had kept pushing on west, hoping to find a spot where he might settle. He had no ties, no connections, but was a homeless wanderer.

After their mid-day meal, the Rio Kid and his two comrades rode on. But Pryor insisted on leaving the haunch of venison with Barron. He and his companions could easily get fresh meat but Barron was not a trained hunter in such country as this, and moreover, could not venture far from his animals.

Barron was taking great care of his horses. He was not riding on immediately now, for he wanted to give them time to graze.

After three hours Barron was left far behind, and the companionable trio were starting down the slope beyond the mountain. New stretches of the mighty, lovely land stretched before them, with smoke hanging in the azure sky miles to their left.

"Settlement," grunted Bigfoot Wallace. "S'pose we keep away from it, Rio Kid? Wild animals don't fancy such, and I reckon we got to bag us an elk, huh."

They cut away from the mountain trail, turning westward along the side of the hill, and pushed on. The sun was dropping, and it was in their eyes, but their ears were keen. And there was no mistaking the sound when they heard several shots faintly, ahead.

"Shucks!" growled Bigfoot. "This country's as crowded as Santa Fé on pay-day, Rio Kid!"

The Rio Kid, out on an uneven, difficult deer trail, cocked his ear to the sounds.

"Quite a scrap over there, if yuh ask me," he remarked.

"Well," complained Wallace, "no self-respectin' antelope in his right mind would hang around here for long. That shootin' shore spiles our huntin'. That Johnny Reb's got our last meat and we won't get no fresh tonight."

Swinging around the huge mountainside, they saw the wooded dip between summits. The shooting was louder in their ears, and the Rio Kid's keen eyes could see the smokepuffs now.

"Say, I just spied an Indian feather!" exclaimed Bigfoot, licking his chops.

"They got somebody treed in that nest of rocks below," the Rio Kid said, nodding.

"If it ain't a private fight," said Wallace, "I'd like to get in it. C'mon!"

Bigfoot had always fought Indians. He still did. He held them off his coach on the six-hundred-mile run from Santa Fé to Austin, driving the mail. He hunted them and bushwhacked them.

"I might even run into that Lipan with the enormous feet over here," he argued. "Yuh never can tell, Rio Kid. Indians travel for miles sometimes."

The going was too rough for any fast riding, and on horseback they would make good targets. Leaving their animals, they started afoot down toward the fray, to see what went on. Each carried a carbine beside his pistols and a knife.

"They're white men down there," the Rio Kid announced after a short while. "Not more than four or five shootin'."

He was on a flat rock, standing up to see over the low-growing piñons on the slope. A bullet suddenly ripped a hole in the crown of his Stetson, and Bigfoot Wallace seized his arm and yanked him down.

"That settles it," growled Bigfoot. "I seen that redskin."

Spread out, the three stalked down the hill.

Wallace's carbine snapped, and then the Rio Kid's.

Bullets zipped in the dry, twisted limbs

23

about them or spattered on the jagged rocks. Moving swiftly, Indian fashion, the trio pushed in, watching for their targets. Now and then, whenever one glimpsed a head-band or a dark face sticking up, he would shoot.

"Navajos, I reckon," muttered Pryor. "Looks like their get-up."

For a time, as they drew closer, the Indians held ground but then they broke as the three scouts showed their fighting ability and accuracy of gun work. They went dashing, bent low, flitting from brush to brush and rock to rock, down across the bottoms and up on the wooded slope beyond.

"Zey have zeir mustangs hidden up in the woods," remarked Celestino as they moved on to the spot deserted by the fleeing Indians.

If the white sharpshooters had killed any of the Indians, then the bodies had been carried off, for they found no corpses on the ground which the enemy had held. The Indians had not given up entirely, either. For long-range fire still came at them. But the bullets flew wild.

"Let 'em go," ordered the Rio Kid, as the savages disappeared over the next ridge and the shooting ceased. "We don't want to foller 'em into that swale of brush and rocks."

A cheer rose from the rock nest where the besieged had been held. The Rio Kid sang out and a man stood up and waved.

"Shucks!" said Bigfoot. "They're Mexes."

Celestino frowned. "Me, too, I'm a Mex, Beegfoot."

Pryor was first at the barricade. A tall young man with a proud face and flashing eyes greeted him in English.

"Good afternoon, sir," he said. "You came at the right moment. Our bullets were just about gone."

He was of Spanish extraction, an educated, intelligent young fellow. Handsome and upstanding. The Rio Kid ticketed him correctly, as soon as he heard him speak, as an American of fine *hidalgo* blood. There were many such in the Southwest.

He wore a red velvet coat and tight riding breeches, with fine boots. A steepled sombrero lay on the ground, with a big tear in it. Blood had run down one cheek, from a scalp injury and his left arm hung limp at his side. He showed no sign of the pain he must have been suffering from his hurts. But his eyes were stricken, and the reason for that was plain when he glanced down at the dead youth who lay at his feet.

"My brother," he said in a voice that broke a little, in answer to the Rio Kid's unspoken

25

question. "He is dead and so is my friend Rafael."

His eyes sought Pryor's, then went on to look into the eyes of Wallace and Mireles as they pushed up, carbines in hand.

Mireles addressed him politely in Spanish, and he replied in the same language.

A seriously wounded young fellow lay unconscious on the other side of the barricade. Two others were trying to staunch the flow of blood from flesh wounds they had received from flying lead and rocks. The wounded men were short, stocky fellows, of *vaquero* stamp, evidently employees of the young fellow who faced the Rio Kid.

"Yore name is Perez," said the Rio Kid, who had heard the young man answer Celestino. For Bob Pryor could speak Spanish as well as his native tongue, being a Border man.

"Yes, I am Manuel Perez. We live at Casa Blanca, a few miles from here."

He waved a fine, long hand in the direction of the smoke they had seen.

"We better start totin' yore brother and these friends of yores back, then," said the Rio Kid.

"Thank you," Perez said.

"If your father," said Celestino in Spanish, "is Don Francisco Perez, then we are distant cousins."

"He is, indeed, Don Francisco," replied Manuel Perez.

They would have to carry the badly injured man. The others could ride, though it took some time to catch their scattered horses. The dead youth was tied to the saddle of one of them, then, and when Mireles hurried away and returned shortly with his pinto, Bigfoot's black, and Saber, Bigfoot carried the wounded man, coddling him gently in his strong arms.

It was dark before they reached the Perez home. There were lights all around, and the Rio Kid could make out the ghostly white shapes of houses that made up what appeared to be a little settlement.

The Perez *hacienda* was a large one, built with overhanging balconies and grilled windows. Wide double doors in the adobe wall opened to receive them and they moved into a great *patio,* where a fountain played among flowering plants. It was paved with stone, and at the rear of the square was a roomy stable. Peons came forward to take care of the horses.

"Manuel!"

A young girl ran from the doorway and threw her arms about Perez's neck. "You — you are hurt! Where's Rafael?"

Even as she asked she saw her other brother, and gave a scream of horror. Weeping, she ran to the horse on which the dead man's corpse was fastened. The men were silent, touched to the heart by her grief.

She was small, with big melting eyes and jet-black hair. Her lovely oval face was beautiful with her soft creamy coloring, and she wore silken clothing and little red slippers.

"Yore wife, Perez?" murmured the Rio Kid.

"No. My sister Dolores. . . . Here is my father, Don Francisco."

The father came slowly down a short fight of steps from the spacious quarters on the second balcony tier. He was a splendid, stalwart man, with curling mustache and dark hair flaked with gray. Wordlessly he took his sobbing daughter in his arms, and stared at his dead son. Then he turned to Manuel.

"Who killed him?"

"Indians, Father. They attacked us without warning while we were hunting and cut us up badly before we could reach cover. They killed Rafael quickly and our followers are wounded. I believe the attackers were Navajos, from what we saw of their head-dress and clothing."

28

"Navajos!" growled Don Francisco. "From the village across the mountain, no doubt." He glanced at the soberly silent Rio Kid and his companions. "Who are these men?" he inquired.

Manuel explained. Don Francisco held out his hand to Pryor.

"You are welcome here, Senor. I will never forget what you have done for us any more than I will forget what the savages have done to my people."

Another woman appeared, an older woman, but still lovely. Donna Rosa, the wife and mother. The Rio Kid did not wish to intrude on the family's grief and led his two friends toward the stables on the pretext of finding water and seeing to their mounts.

After a time Manuel appeared, searching for them. He begged them to come to the private apartments of the Perez family across the flagged *patio*.

A murmur of excitement stirred the *hacienda* by now. Angry retainers and friends were infuriated by the Indian outrage.

Bigfoot Wallace had wandered off to the big kitchen and was busy filling himself while he regaled a large-eyed cook with tales of his prowess. Celestino silently followed the Rio Kid to the great main room of the house.

The mother and sister of the dead youth did not again appear, but remained in their rooms. Attendants had fetched in wine and other refreshments, and Don Francisco Perez and his son Manuel, the latter having washed the blood from himself and changed to fresh clothing, welcomed their guests. The Rio Kid's quick eye took in the beautiful antiques with which the cool, thick-walled place was furnished.

Father and son had full control of their grief now, though they were quiet and steady-eyed. Both had the manners and courtesy of gentlemen born. They were fine people, thought Pryor.

"The Navajos shall pay for what they have done," promised Don Francisco.

As a soldier, officer and fighting man — the don and his son soon discovered that — they held the Rio Kid in the highest esteem. Besides his aid to Manuel had endeared him to them. They insisted that he and his friends should at least remain overnight.

Worn out by hard riding and the battle in the mountains, the Rio Kid turned in early. They were given a large suite off the *patio,* with great bedsteads and fine rugs. Celestino had dwelt in such a home as a boy, before bandits had scourged and destroyed his family and ranch, and though it all

30

brought a lump to his throat, he was accustomed to it.

But Bigfoot Wallace was astonished by the luxuries. He tossed for an hour on his bed, then the Rio Kid heard him cursing as Bigfoot took his blanket outside and lay down on the stones. He was not used to a spring and mattresses.

Chapter III
Another Rescue

Young Arthur Barron started awake, ears wide. During the War he had learned how to bivouac anywhere he chanced to be, so it was not discomfort that had aroused him. The hard earth made a good bed when a man was used to it, so it was not the stones under his body which had brought him wide awake.

He could hear the soft stampings of his prized horses, the snort of the handsome big stallion. He had them in a natural pen formed by rock cliff walls, easy enough to find in these hills. There was but one open side to it, and across that he had stretched a lariat which the horses would not pass.

With his horses in mind, Barron listened intently. The wind blew draughtily through the gap, and the sough of it in the dry brush made it difficult to distinguish anything.

And he was worried about those horses — all he had. For life had not been easy for the young Kentuckian. At the age of eighteen he had gone off to the War, and through it had lost all he had been brought up to. He had not yet found a haven, as he had hunted for a fresh start.

His money was used up now, and the Confederate currency he still had was useless. His food was about gone. He could sell his horses but that would be only as a last resort, and would kill his hope of fortune. He had looked forward, somehow, to raising blooded animals from the bunch.

A stone rolled near at hand and he peered at the dense blackness of the cliff wall.

Against the sky he saw a feather sticking up. Then it was gone. Swiftly he reached for his Army pistol, loaded and ready at his side. As he shifted his position, guns flared, and lead slugs bit into the blanket where he had been lying. One tore a gash in his thigh, a wound that hurt horribly, but he threw up his revolver and answered.

They seemed to be all around him, their shrill whoops ringing in the confined space. He ran, limping because of his wounded side, to the left, only to have several blanketed men rise up before him and shoot his way. He swung to the other flank, seeking escape, but they were after him, his progress blocked.

Another bullet ripped into his shoulder and spun him half around. The shock dropped him to his knee. He pulled his trigger as fast as he could, letting go at the shadowy attackers.

He was driven back to the rope which held his animals in. He recognized the sound made by his gray, whinnying in alarm, and the horses were milling around, frightened by the heavy gunfire so close at hand.

"They're after my horses!" he thought, in a confused nightmare, but the marauders came on, hunting him in the blackness.

He was bleeding profusely, for the slugs had not only hurt him but had half stunned him. Somehow, though, he managed to get to the natural pen, ducked under the confining lariat and got hold of Greyboy's long mane with his left hand. Staggering, he managed to pull himself across the animal's back.

Greyboy was frantic with terror, jerking his head around, stamping.

Dark figures flew at Barron, reaching for Greyboy to stop his escape. Barron fired at the closest of them, and heard a shrill scream, an oath.

Then the lariat keeping the band of Kentucky horses penned, either broke or was cut, and the maddened animals rushed out.

Something zipped past Barron's ear. He went limp, flopped over Greyboy's back, with a hand wound in the mane. A bullet had hit Arthur Barron's skull. . . .

Meanwhile, in the Perez *hacienda* the Rio Kid was up early, refreshed and starving for food. Bigfoot Wallace who had slept outside had already risen.

After breakfast, Pryor strolled outside. In the fresh morning light he could now take in the surroundings. The Perez *hacienda* stood on a hillside, shaded by live-oaks, and near at hand was a village. Tilled fields were here, and pastures in which ran cattle and horses.

There were smaller homes about the plaza, on which grazed sheep and goats. *Vaqueros* and field workers with their families lived in these smaller adobe houses. And there were still other abodes, larger places on the surrounding slopes. No doubt, the Rio Kid surmised, these homes were occupied by neighbors and friends of the Perez family.

"Fine folks," grunted someone, coming up behind him. "But they ain't practical. They'll lose all they got."

It was Bigfoot Wallace, stuffed to repletion.

The Rio Kid nodded. Just two decades ago, he knew, this had been part of Mexico. In 1848 it had been ceded to the United States along with its inhabitants. People like the Perez family had become American citizens. They kept on living as they always had, in a leisurely, pastoral fashion, with plenty of food for all raised in the fields, the vineyards, and on the range. But they had no idea of business as practiced by the bustling Yankees.

Across the square stood a beautiful, tall-steepled church. In the center of the commons was a public fountain and watering-trough, fed from ice-cold mountain springs. The sun gleamed with dazzling splendor on the whitewashed adobe walls of the buildings.

A bell began to toll, and men in leather riding clothes, armed with pistols and knives, many carrying rifles as well, appeared from the barns and stables, leading saddled horses with them.

There were some fifty of these fighters. Many were of Spanish descent, *vaqueros,* but there were plain Americans also, for several families in the littte town had come from New England and the Middle Atlantic States, choosing to settle down among the *haciendas* and their kind inhabitants.

Manuel Perez emerged, and nodded to the Rio Kid and his companion.

"We are going hunting," he remarked grimly.

"After Indians?" asked Wallace.

"*Si*. After those who attacked us — the Navajos."

"Good!" exclaimed Wallace. "C'mon, Rio Kid. It's more sport than huntin' elk. Saddle up that moth-eaten dun of yores and we'll ride along."

"There are some things to be done, before we can start," Manuel put in. "My father is sending a warning to the Indian Commissioner in charge of the Navajos. He lives at Taos, not far from here."

"Old Kit Carson!" Bigfoot cried. "He's a pard of mine. But he loves Indians, 'less they're on the warpath."

The Rio Kid had heard of Kit Carson, the famous scout and trapper. John Charles Frémont, for whom Carson had guided during his majestic and vital exploring trips in the West two decades before, had been much in the public eye lately.

Before the Civil War, Frémont had run for President against Buchanan, and there had been talk of Frémont as candidate of an opposition party to Abraham Lincoln although this had never been carried through. As an explorer, however, Frémont had been a giant, a genius. It was to him that the acquisition of California by the United States was chiefly due.

But after this great work was ended, Fremont's luck had run out. He had been a general in the Civil War but, daring to go against orders, had actually been court-martialed and dismissed from the army he had served so well. His political life had been unhappy as well.

Yet throughout the new States and the Territories the name of Kit Carson, Frémont's chief guide and friend, was already legendary. Carson, still trapping now and then, was nearing sixty, but he was active and had been appointed Indian agent to the Utes, Apaches and Navajos in the Taos district.

"I'd shore like to shake hands with Kit Carson," said the Rio Kid.

"If you come back with us, he should be here," Manuel Perez replied. "The Indians call him Father Kit, because he has been very good to them. But he will fight them if they insist on being bad."

A messenger was dispatched to Taos, with a letter from Don Francisco to Kit Carson. Arms were being checked and ammunition passed around. Bundles of blanket rolls and food were made ready.

As they were preparing to start, with Don Francisco acting as their captain, there was a hubbub at the end of the town. Several men came along escorting a peon, a stocky, black-haired fellow who was part Indian and part Mexican. He was one of Perez' sheepherders and was leading a horse.

"What is it, Pablo?" inquired Don Francisco.

"Don Francisco, while I was eating my breakfast," replied Pablo in his native tongue, "the dog barked and I looked up and saw a man lying across a horse. He was wounded, and I have brought him here."

The Rio Kid looked at the unconscious figure on the back of the bedraggled, bloodstained animal which Pablo had led in, and his eyes opened wide with surprise.

"Say — I've seen that hoss before," he muttered, pushing closer.

And the next moment his recognition of the horse was complete. It was Greyboy, Arthur Barron's mount, and the limp man lying on him, a death grip on Greyboy's silky mane, was Barron.

"Well, I'll be dogged if it ain't the Johnny Reb!" cried Bigfoot Wallace.

Greyboy had two bullet creases, bloody and scabbing, in his once-sleek hide. Burrs were thick in his tail and coat, and he had picked up a stone and gone lame in a foreleg. He was worn out from running and in need of attention.

Don Francisco, who loved horses and had an eye for them, gave orders that Greyboy was to be cared for at once.

The Rio Kid, assisted by Wallace, lifted Barron to the ground and stretched him out.

"He's dead," declared Bigfoot, but the Rio Kid shook his head.

"No, he ain't. Not unless ghosts kin talk."

"Indians — Indians!" whispered Barron, his eyelids flickering.

Kneeling beside him, the Rio Kid hunted for the wounds. He found a torn thigh, and a wounded shoulder from which the bullet had not emerged. There was, as well, a head injury. Pryor could not tell the extent of that from a superficial examination.

"Take him inside," Perez commanded.

They carried Barron into the *hacienda*. Donna Rosa and her women servants would attend to him. Everything possible would be done to fan the spark of life remaining in him.

"They must've spotted them hosses," said Bigfoot, "and laid for him last night, Rio Kid. Most anybody would give his right eye for a bunch like Barron had. Well, they're gone now. The Navajo bucks'll ride 'em to death."

The mustangs of the Indian hunting party were fresh, dancing about in excitement, ready for the run. The band under Don Francisco was as impatient to start as the animals, and soon he took the lead and rode forth from Valcito, as the settlement was called. They swung southwest on a beaten trail toward the village of the Navajos, determined to avenge the murders of their sons and the unprovoked attacks.

The Rio Kid scouted ahead. When it was nearing noon and they had come many miles from Valcito, he saw a large number of riders coming toward them. After a quick glance, he turned and spurred back to report.

"There's a couple of hundred Indians headin' this way, Don Francisco. I think they're Navajos but I ain't shore what tribal branch. They're armed with rifles and look like they're huntin' trouble."

"Good!" said Perez grimly, his bearded jaw setting. "We'll attack."

He swung in his single-fire saddle — he rode a single cinch rig, California style — and sang out to his men to make ready to fight.

The little army started forward at an increased pace, guns loaded and raised. The Indians came more slowly, spreading out as they saw the white men. They were carrying Government-issue rifles.

"*Si*, they are Navajos, from the very village I suspected," growled Don Perez.

"They're on the warpath for fair," cried Bigfoot Wallace. "Drop them guns!" he roared, his voice bellowing in the shallow depression across which the two parties approached one another.

The Indians were big, dark-skinned fellows, some in leather, others wearing headbands such as the Apaches sported. Their bronzed, greased torsos gleamed.

An excited member of Perez' party fired a shot from his revolver at the Navajos. At the shot, the Navajos instantly reined in their horses and throwing carbines to shoulders, replied in kind. Bullets shrieked about the Rio Kid, Don Francisco and Manuel, who were in the van. A man at Bigfoot Wallace's side swore and jumped in his saddle, a slug burning his flesh.

"Fire!" roared Perez.

Now they shot to kill. The range was long, but one Indian crashed dead from his saddle, while several others felt lead.

"Charge!" ordered Don Francisco.

CHAPTER IV
INDIAN HUNTERS

Spurting forward on Saber, the Rio Kid led the attack. Bullets were thick in the mountain air but the Navajos, after letting loose a second hurried volley, refused to stand. They split up into small groups, riding off in every direction through the thick bush.

It became a matter of running, individual pursuits, a white chasing a buck or two, trying to get close enough for a fair shot at the elusive Indians. The Navajos had a genius for disappearing, and they were expert riders.

After an hour of dodging through thorny chaparral, the Perez party reformed on the trail, their horses lathered and torn by long thorns.

"Let's push on to their village, Father," suggested Manuel Perez. "We'll never overtake them in the brush."

"*Bueno.* First we'll drink and have a quick bite."

"Who fired that first shot from our bunch?" demanded the Rio Kid.

No one answered for a moment. Then someone said:

"It was Gasca."

"Stand forth, Gasca," Perez ordered.

A dark-faced *vaquero* in leather, one of Don Perez' employes, stepped out. The Rio Kid coolly looked him over. Gasca, armed with a knife and pistol, wore high leather boots; and a curved gray sombrero. His eyes were inkspots in yellow pools, his nose flat and bridgeless. He grinned, showing a broken front tooth.

"A thousand pardons, Senors," he said in Spanish. "It was one of my cousins who died yesterday out with Don Manuel. I hate the Navajos."

"Don't go off half-cocked again, Gasca," the Rio Kid said.

"Oh well," Don Francisco shrugged — "no doubt they would have opened fire on us in a moment anyway, no matter what Gasca or any of us did. They were evidently headed toward our homes to do mischief, otherwise they wouldn't have been so ready and quick to fight."

Soon they rode on, westward, over the mountain, and below them stood the Navajo village. Spurring down the slope, they rushed into the place whooping it up, but it was deserted.

Empty hogans, made of brush, rock and stretched hide, stood about. There were evidences that the tribe had made a hurried departure. ∽

"They have driven their flocks and horses into the mountain fastnesses where we can't get at them," growled Don Perez. "The women and children and old men have charge of the animals and supplies while the braves are on the warpath. It means real trouble. We'll never be safe, *amigos,* till they're rounded up."

Several hot-headed fellows lighted torches and set fire to the hogans, which burned with an evil stench of singed hide.

Distant rifles opened up from the sides of the hills, and bullets, almost spent, plunked among the white attackers. Mounting again, they headed up at the Indians, only to find they had melted off by the time they arrived.

After fruitless pursuit, Don Francisco turned his weary men for home. It was after dark when they pulled into Valcito, splitting up and going to their various homes.

The Rio Kid, Mireles and Bigfoot Wallace went into the big *hacienda* with Manuel and his father. A man was awaiting Perez, standing in the middle of the salon, watching them as they entered.

He was about five-feet-six, certainly not an imposing figure. He had a slender body, and his sandy hair was frosted at the temples. His face was freckled. The eyes, gray-blue and twinkling with intense life, were magnetic.

The large head showed intelligence. A high brow, a broad nose, slightly retroussé, a deep chest, helped complete his physical attributes. His wiry body was clad in buckskin, soft stuff that clung to the sinews.

"Good evening, Don Francisco," he said. His voice was soft and caressing.

"Good evening! Senor Carson, do you know my friends? This is Senor Pryor, whom they call the Rio Kid."

Captain Pryor stepped forward. The sagacious gray-blue eyes fixed his, measuring him. And then Kit Carson shook his hand.

The Rio Kid was too astonished to speak for a moment. Kit Carson's appearance was such a contrast to his reputation. For so startlingly brave a person, Carson looked fragile, his physical self not approaching the giant size of his character. A modest and naturally refined man, he always shrank from public notice.

Yet the Rio Kid was aware that Kit Carson was a Titan, one of the great who had driven the wedges that spread the United States from ocean to ocean. He was in the same class with Daniel Boone and Bowie.

Stories of Kit Carson's intrepidity as a scout and trapper were countless. In his 'teens he had already been a pioneer, breaking new trails to the great, unknown West. He had fought Indians up and down across the land. With John Frémont he had added thousands of square miles to the growing country, and was himself an explorer of renown. Had it not been for Carson, Frémont might never have so brilliantly succeeded.

During the Civil War, Kit Carson had been a brigadier-general for the Union, helped hold the Southwest for Lincoln. Though nearing sixty, Kit Carson was still as good as ever, mentally and physically; the Rio Kid could feel the sinews of steel in his hand.

All of this sped through Bob Pryor's mind like lightning, as he cried, gripping the great scout's hand:

"This *is* a pleasure, Kit Carson!"

It was late at night, and most of the little settlement where the Rio Kid and his companions had paused when they had ridden into New Mexico had long ago taken to their beds.

The *Gazette* office and Hannigan's store were dark, as were the surrounding homes. But lights showed in the side windows at the rear of the building with its double purpose.

Several rough-looking fellows, riders for the big rancher, Ole Stensen, who had felt the weight of the Rio Kid's pile-driver fist, were drinking and playing cards at a table in the kitchen where a single lamp burned. Hannigan, the storekeeper-editor, Stensen, and a third man were in the living room, talking things over in low voices.

Hannigan was slumped in his big chair by the fire of piñon knots — for the mountain air cooled rapidly when the sun went down — was listening to the other two men. Or rather, to the big rancher who at the moment had the floor. Ole Stensen was wearing buckskin now, instead of his usual cowboy garb, and berry stain darkened his weather-beaten face to a coppery shade. He was grinning as he said:

"We got them hosses, and they're beauties, Jed. I sent the boys on to the ranch with 'em."

"Did yuh get the man, too?" Hannigan growled, a frown accenting the beadiness of his eyes.

"Oh, shore," boasted Stensen. "We riddled

him, Jed. He couldn't have gone more'n a mile of two 'fore he died."

Hannigan's scowl grew deeper. "What yuh mean, 'fore he died?" he demanded. "Don't yuh know where he fell?"

"Not exactly. It was night, remember, and he managed to throw hisself over his cayuse and the animal went wild and run. But he's done for, for fair. I guarantee it. My last bullet hit him in the head."

"Yuh lost that gray he was ridin'? It was worth a thousand dollars if it was worth two bits."

"Well, one of us'll pick it up 'fore long. Barron's coyote bait."

The third man in that conference was a half-breed, half Mexican, half Apache Indian, a man who had inherited the worst characteristics of both races. He had a mis-shapen head and was known locally as "Egghead Pete." Though not large in body he was as sinewy as a cougar, the corded muscles standing out grotesquely from the flesh. His legs were as bowed as a wedding ring.

No one knew his real name, if he did himself. But he had an evil intelligence and deep cunning which made him a valuable tool. He was utterly ruthless.

His dull-black eyes were almost Oriental,

slitted and with an upward tilt. Two brown lines passed for lips to the mouth that was small and straight. His ears stuck out at right angles to his head, the lusterless ebony locks bound by a dirty white head-band, Apache style.

He wore doeskin pants, with fringes at the edges, a cotton shirt, and beaded moccasins with uppers that came to his knees to ward off thorns. A knife was in his sash, and a Colt revolver in a new holster was a present from his employer, Hannigan. He carried his bullets in his pockets rather than in a belt.

"Today dey fight," growled Egghead, when Stensen had finished his report. "*Si,* dey fight," he repeated in his hoarse, monotonous voice. "I was dere, weeth the Navajos, and dere's no doubt now. It's war, majordomo."

"Good work, Pete," Hannigan congratulated. "Yuh've done more'n any of us."

CHAPTER V
PARLEY

Cleverly had Egghead Pete worked up the trouble between the settlers of Valcito and the Navajos, their neighbors. In the dark shadows outside of the store now were several of his renegades, Apache and Navajo criminals he had enlisted.

He had dressed them as Navajos and had attacked Manuel Perez and his friends. Then some of Stensen's white cronies, from his ranch, had massacred a small party of Navajo herders, peacefully going about their work. Egghead Pete and his men had carried the corpses back to the Navajo village, reporting that it was the work of the whites, that the men of Valcito intended to drive the Navajos from their reservation and seize their flocks and land.

The childlike Navajos had believed the stories almost fully. They had started their animals off into the mountains, with their women and children, while fighters had armed themselves and headed to Valcito to make certain it was war. Stensen's killers had made sure a clear white-man's trail led to Valcito.

Jed Hannigan had planned it all, but Egghead Pete and Stensen had carried out his bidding to the letter.

Hannigan rubbed his hands together, a twisted smile on his lips.

"We got 'em started now," he declared, "and they'll wear each other down. All we got to do is make shore they don't patch up a peace. That should be a cinch. We —" He broke off, cocking his head to listen. "Somebody's comin'," he said.

It was the beat of hoofs he had heard. Soon the sound grew louder and a rider swung in to the store, coming more slowly down the side to the back door.

Hannigan got up and went through the kitchen. The waddies did not look up from their cards as he passed. He flung open the door and the beam from the oil lamp on the table showed a man dismounting from a heaving, lathered horse, its flanks bleeding from deep and cruel spur gouges.

"Telesforo!" exclaimed Hannigan. "What's up?"

"I've come to report, Senor Hannigan."

The rider came inside, quirt flapping

against his leather-clad leg. And his appearance there would have been a shock to the men of Valcito. For he was Telesforo Gasca, the *vaquero* who rode for Don Francisco Perez. In reality he had been sent to Valcito by Jed Hannigan as a spy.

After a drink, he made his report.

"Perez and all believe now that the Navajos are responsible," he informed Hannigan. "We met them yesterday and there was a skirmish, which I cleverly began by firing a shot."

Egghead Pete nodded. "*Si,* dat's right, majordomo. Gasca fired."

"Pete told me," Hannigan said. "Why did yuh come here tonight, Telesforo?"

"It was to tell you that Perez has sent for Kit Carson."

"I thought he would," grunted Hannigan.

"Others have come to the *hacienda,* as well. One known as 'Bigfoot', the other the Rio Kid. They can fight, and like madmen."

"Ugh!" growled Hannigan, blinking. "They were the ones who horned in on our game with that Johnny Reb who had the hosses."

Gasca took another swig from the bottle at hand, and wiped his mouth with the back of a bronzed hand.

"There's another, too," he added casually.

53

"He was fetched in by one of Don Francisco's sheepherders. 'Bar-ron,' he is called. He lost some horses and —"

"What!"

Jed Hannigan cast a furious glance at Stensen, who swore in confusion.

"So he couldn't have ridden a mile!" snarled Hannigan. "Yuh fool, Ole, he got away!"

"Shucks, I was shore —" began Stensen, but Hannigan stopped him short.

Hannigan began to question Gasca, who replied, with a shrug:

"I can't say whether he'll live or not. He's in the *hacienda* and the women are caring for him."

Hannigan got up, paced the floor, his hands clasped behind his back.

"I better ride over there tomorrow," he announced at last. "I want to see Perez, anyway. There's no tellin' what that Johnny Reb may remember when he comes to. If he shows 'em where Stensen stole them hosses they may backtrack and figger white men did it. We'll make shore he don't talk. I'll check on Kit Carson, too."

"Cuss yuh, Ole, we can't sell them hosses now, unless we drive them way off. Hold 'em at yore ranch, savvy? There's five thousand in 'em and I could use some extra

54

cash. Keep yore boys busy. Perez will pull his *vaqueros* in off the range and so'll everybody else in Valcito, and yuh'll have clear sailin'. Yuh can run off as much stock as yuh like."

He dismissed his lieutenants with a peremptory wave of his hand. Gasca took a final drink, and went out to the stable to saddle up a fresh mustang for his return trip to Valcito. Stensen called his waddies and they set out for his ranch, the Circle S, a few miles from the settlement.

Egghead Pete simply melted away in the night. He was supposed to head back into the wilds with his renegades and keep tab on the Navajos, luckless victims, with Perez and his friends, of Jed Hannigan's greedy ambitions.

Hannigan blew out the lamps, went to his bunk and lay down. For a time he stared at the dark ceiling rafters, frowning as he thought out his plans.

They were large. He was a petty but conniving Territorial politician, and to achieve his ambitions he needed money, not the few thousands he had made by purchasing cheap goods and selling them at exorbitant profits to the Indians and needy settlers who had to be given credit.

What he wanted was real money. His idea

of politics was to have plenty of cash with which to grease hands on the boost up. And, in that time, there were many who rose to the top in such fashion. In the back of his agile brain burned a consuming desire to be New Mexico's first governor when she was admitted to the Union as a state.

The robbing of Arthur Barron had been but a small incident. Hannigan, however, never allowed anything as easy and as good as that to slip through his hands.

He had to keep Stensen and his men satisfied; also Egghead Pete. The drygulching, evidently by Indians, of a friendless wanderer, a Johnny Reb as Hannigan had taken care to point out to the citizens, would have roused little interest, and the horses were worth good money.

He had no intention of permitting anyone to interfere with his plans. . . .

At about the same time other men, some distance away, in Valcito, were wide awake and considering plans of their own. In Don Perez' *hacienda* Kit Carson was in earnest consultation with Don Francisco, Manuel Perez, the Rio Kid and his two companions, over what on the surface appeared to be an Indian uprising. The idea pained Kit Carson, but he was never a man to shirk an obvious duty facing him.

"We will fight them," Carson said in his well-modulated voice, "if they insist, Don Perez. But think first. Is it the right course to take without givin' 'em a chance to parley? There may be some mistake."

"Mistake!" exclaimed Don Francisco. "Could they have killed my son and my neighbors by mistake? And didn't they open fire on us? Remember this, Senor Carson — they had already sent their women and stock into the mountains, which means they intended to go on the warpath."

Kit Carson's gray-blue eyes were grave. He stroked his chin thoughtfully. He preferred to weigh every move, to consider whether it might be ethical or not before leaping into action.

Carson had a deep sympathy for all Indians. He understood them and had always tried to help them with their problems. He was known as one of the greatest of Indian fighters but this was necessary in order to hold the respect of the savages. They cared nothing for a man who would not stand up and fight for his rights.

But it was his way to try diplomacy first, with fighting a last resort, and the trust the Indians put in him was tremendous. He was "Father Kit" to them.

"Is it right for us to pursue 'em and attack 'em?" he asked thoughtfully. "Ought we to do this? You know what human nature is, gentlemen. Once we set out after 'em, there'll be no turnin' back."

Don Perez shrugged. Like all his friends, he was convinced that the Navajos must be pursued to the end and shattered.

"Shucks," growled Bigfoot Wallace, winking an eye. "The only good Injun's a dead one, Kit. Let's reform 'em. That's my motto."

Carson shook his head sadly.

"Friend Bigfoot, yuh're a good man and I know yuh believe yuh're right. But yuh should think first in the Indian matter."

"What?" exploded Bigfoot. "Think, with a rip-roarin', murderin' son-of-a-gun howlin' on my trail, with his scalpin' knife up? If I done thought then, Kit, it would be my last try. Kill 'em first and argufy afterwards."

The Rio Kid was silent. He was impressed by Kit Carson and well aware that the great scout was much better acquainted with the Indian problem than perhaps anyone else in the West. Carson had married into an Indian tribe and had lived among them all his life. He had helped them, fought them, and was an expert at soothing the redskins.

"Sometimes," said Kit Carson, speaking

to his host, "it's better to get along with yore neighbors than it is to fight 'em, Don Perez."

"They've attacked us, not once but several times," Don Francisco said grimly. "We would be fools not to protect ourselves."

"Well," Carson agreed slowly, "make yore preparations. I'll try one more stab at talkin' 'em into their senses."

"How?" demanded Perez.

"I'll ride up into the mountains and visit 'em in their stronghold. I ain't had much to do with this tribe, but I savvy their chief, Wolfkiller."

Don Francisco and the other men in the room stared disbelievingly at Kit Carson.

"But — that would mean sure death!" exclaimed Perez. "To ride alone in their camp, when they're on the warpath, is suicide!"

The Rio Kid was watching the calm, high-browed face of the Indian agent. Kit Carson meant what he said.

"Take me with yuh, Kit?" the Rio Kid suddenly asked.

It was Kit Carson's turn to measure the Rio Kid. He seemed about to shake his fine head, but then he nodded.

"If yuh want to come, all right. But no more than the two of us. It would be a challenge if a big party horned in. What Don Francisco says is true. It's dangerous. If yuh ain't shore yuh want to go, why, it's all right."

"I'm ready any time," the Rio Kid declared.

A *vaquero* appeared at the open door.

"Don Francisco, Senor Hannigan has come!"

The Rio Kid turned. He recognized Jed Hannigan, the storekeeper with whom he had had the little brush in defending Arthur Barron. Hannigan had on a sweeping black coat.

"Howdy, Don Francisco!" Hannigan cried heartily. "It's a sight for sore eyes to see yuh again!"

He thrust his hand into Perez' and pumped his arm. He was effusive, almost fawning on the wealthy don.

"Heard yuh was havin' some Injun trouble, the dirty red varmints. Sooner the country's cleaned of the devils, the better, say I. I've printed that in my paper every issue since I brought her out. Mighty sorry about yore boy that got kilt. He was a fine young feller. If there's anything I can do for yuh now —"

Don Perez frowned, drawing back from Hannigan's pawing.

"*Si, si,*" he said shortly. "I will need supplies, a great many. Bullets and new guns, food. We are equipping a small army to enter the mountains and destroy the Navajos who attacked us."

"Everything I got is yores," Hannigan promised. "Give me a list of what yuh need."

The Rio Kid got up from his chair, and strolled over.

"Howdy, Hannigan," he drawled. "Yuh're in a better humor today."

Hannigan swung, and the fatuous smile left his lips for a moment as he recognized the Rio Kid.

"So you're here," he remarked.

"My friend, my *good* friend, *Capitano* Pryor, Hannigan," said Don Francisco coolly.

"A friend of the don's is a friend of mine," Hannigan cried. "Put her there, Rio Kid!"

The Rio Kid pretended not to see Hannigan's outthrust hand. "It's close in here," he said. "I reckon I'll step out into the *patio.*"

He had no desire to be friendly with a man who was cruel to the luckless and poor, and subservient to the wealthy, as Hannigan was. He was thinking of Arthur Barron, too, and his thoughts were grim. It would

be a good idea now, he decided, to see how
Barron was coming on.

CHAPTER VI
WAR

When the Rio Kid had looked in on Barron earlier, the young man had been conscious but weak, too weak to talk much. Barron was in a small apartment off to the right, on the ground floor. The door was open, and the Rio Kid stepped inside, partially blinded by the strong sunlight that came into the *patio.*

"Hello, Rio Kid!" Barron said. His voice was stronger.

Pretty Senorita Dolores Perez stood at the side of the bed. Two older women were also in the room, one of them Donna Rosa, the other a servant. The three had brought warm broth and other foods to tempt the wounded stranger. Under such sympathetic ministrations Arthur Barron had taken some nourishment and felt better. He managed a one-sided smile as Bob Pryor came over and stood beside his couch.

The room was spacious, and cool, with

whitewashed walls adorned with tapestries, a fireplace, Navajo rugs, and heavy, austere furniture. There were two windows both giving onto the *patio*. The outside wall was blank save for a narrow barred slit, really a loophole through which to thrust a rifle in a siege.

"He is splendid," Senorita Dolores said in her sweet voice.

She smiled and her dark eyes lighted. Barron watched her with a grateful light in his eyes. Admiration was there, also, for she was exquisite, in the dress of her people.

A few words were spoken to the Rio Kid by Donna Rosa, then she and her lovely daughter and the woman servant left.

When they were gone, the Rio Kid sat down and offered Barron a cigarette. Barron wore a bandage on one side of his head, and others swathed the wounds in his body.

"Yuh really pickin' up?" the Rio Kid asked.

"Yes," replied Barron. "I still feel mighty weak, like a kitten. But I'll pull through, I know it. And I'll get back my horses." He looked straight into the Rio Kid's eyes. "Greyboy?"

The Rio Kid knew how a man felt about his favorite horse.

"I took a look at him 'fore breakfast," he

said. "He's goin' to be all right, Barron. Needs attention and rest, though."

Barron heaved a deep sigh of relief. "Now I can lie easy."

"Indians hit yuh, huh?" said the Rio Kid. "They must've picked up yore trail 'fore dark and marked yore bivouac, eh?"

Barron nodded. "After you left, I went on slowly, and found a good place to camp. I was sleepin' when they attacked. I saw some feathered heads, though, and knew the attackers were Indians."

"Could yuh say what tribe they were? See any markin's? But I reckon it was too dark."

"Yeah, it was too dark for that. Anyway, I wouldn't know one tribe from another in broad daylight! I don't know a thing about Indians, Rio Kid. I shot one, I'm sure of that. He was screaming like a baby and swearin'."

"He was what?"

"Swearin'."

"Wait! Yuh said he was screamin'. How did he scream?"

"Why, the way anybody would," Barron said, puzzled.

"Huh. He swore, too? What'd he say?"

"Well, all I remember is 'danged lobo'."

The Rio Kid was puzzled. "He might've been a mission Indian, I s'pose. But even that kind don't yell the way a white man does, when he's hurt. 'Ai-ai-ai,' they sometimes go."

He rose. It was plain that Barron was weary, needed lots of sleep. The young fellow's eyelids were drooping and pain racked him.

"When I have time, I'll go back and take a look where that attack was," he said. "How far from where we left yuh were yuh when yore hosses were stolen?"

Barron described the cut and little side niche where he had camped. The Rio Kid swung, and went outside. He would do what he could for Arthur Barron, of course, but the loss of a band of horses was a small matter compared to what was before him.

He meant to ride with Kit Carson at dawn the next day, headed for the mountains where the Navajos had fled. It was known that roving tribes of Apaches were down that way, and the Navajos would sometimes enlist their cousins, the fierce ones, in such a war. The Apaches would be glad to throw in with their red relatives. It would not do, in case Perez and his friends meant to go all the way, not to be fully prepared to meet five hundred or a thousand braves.

He spent the rest of the day grooming Saber, checking his arms and gear. He mended a loose seam in a stirrup strap.

Jed Hannigan was around, but the Rio Kid avoided his vicinity. Francisco Perez and his friends were making full and careful preparations for their expedition against the Indians, and Hannigan would supply much of the needed material from his store. But the Rio Kid wanted no personal contact with the man.

Late in the afternoon, gunshots rang out. The alarm bell tolled, and armed men rushed forth, ready for a fight. Navajos were up on the mountainside, shooting rifles down into the town.

Perez led his mounted followers up at them but they faded away into the rocks and brush.

And at dark a dead sheepherder, his head a horrible mess where he had been scalped alive, was brought in on a cart by a *vaquero.* Such an occurrence, of course, made it necessary to keep alert guards around the town to prevent any night raid.

The Rio Kid ate dinner with the Perez family. Kit Carson and Mireles were also their guests. Jed Hannigan was not present, for though he was still at the *hacienda* Don Perez had not invited him to the inner circle. He was somewhere else in the great establishment. The Rio Kid was not interested where, so long as he did not have to break bread with the man. . . .

Hannigan had his meal in the huge main quarters where the *vaqueros* and numerous other followers of the Perez family gathered. Telesforo Gasca, too, was present, but he and the storekeeper kept apart. Not until he had finished his food and smoke did Hannigan glance at Gasca, rise, and stroll out one of the rear doors.

He waited down the wall, in the dense shadow, and soon Gasca followed him.

"Gasca — here I am," Hannigan, voice low, called.

"*Si,* majordomo."

Gasca slid up to him.

Hannigan was in an evil humor.

"I ain't good enough to sit down to table with 'em," he grumbled. "Perez treats me like a servant, blast him. But I'll show him. I'll teach these cussed dons a lesson they won't forget."

Gasca shrugged. He spoke in Spanish, for his English was none too good.

"You hear the talk, what Bar-ron say?"

"No. What is it?"

"I was leaning against the wall, smoking a cigarette, close to the open window when the Rio Kid spoke with him. He's better. And the Rio Kid wonders at the way those

68

Indians wailed, the ones who attacked Barron."

Hannigan swore. "I knew it! Barron is a cussed nuisance. The Rio Kid, too. Now listen carefully, Gasca. I have two things for yuh to do, right away. First, slide a knife into Barron's heart tonight. When yuh've finished him, saddle the best hoss here and ride. Find Egghead, and tell him that Kit Carson and the Rio Kid are startin' for the Navajos' mountain hideout at dawn. They're not to reach it, savvy, not by any stretch. Egghead must drygulch 'em on their way in."

"Where to find him?" asked Gasca.

"You know Skeleton Peak, ten miles south of here? Head for it, and build a fire of piñon knots on the west side. Egghead will come to yuh, as soon as he can. It's a signal we agreed on. He's somewheres in the mountains with his men."

"Bueno."

"You'll have to wait till the *hacienda* quiets down, 'fore yuh go after Barron. Make no fuss about it, and then get goin'."

Gasca nodded. Hannigan slipped him some money, and they parted, Gasca going to the stables to make ready his mustang, while Hannigan returned to the light and warmth of the great kitchens. . . .

The Rio Kid, aware that he must be up at dawn to begin the dangerous run to the stronghold of the infuriated Indians, with his friend Kit Carson, turned in soon after the evening meal, and fell asleep at once in his comfortable bed.

Bigfoot Wallace, who was chagrined at being left behind — for nothing would induce Carson to let anyone else but the Rio Kid accompany him on his mission — stalked into a nearby room. He kept trying to bunk in the fine bed allotted him, but he hadn't had any luck so far. He was determined, however, to fight it out even if he went without sleep every night he was here.

In only a short time Pryor came to his senses with that sudden, familiar start. He was alert, fully prepared for anything.

The *hacienda* was dark, and quiet, and someone was close to him. His hand tightened on the revolver which never left his side, at night or during the day.

"Hey, Rio Kid!" It was his crony, Bigfoot Wallace.

"What's up?" whispered Pryor.

"Ssh — keep it quiet. Get up and foller me."

The Rio Kid knew the big scout too well to ask questions then. He slid from his couch, his bare feet making no sounds.

Wallace led him to the open door which gave onto the big *patio,* and touched the Rio Kid's arm.

"An hombre just crawled in Barron's winder," Bigfoot told him. "I couldn't sleep as usual in that there mess of fluff, and so I give up and went out to lie on the stones. I was in the shadows, and just now I seen him. Thought I better get you. I don't savvy the politics in this here place —"

"Yuh able to reckernize who it was?"

"No, but he was dressed like a *vaquero.* Come from the stable way, snuk around some to make shore the coast was clear, and then clumb like a snake through Barron's open winder. Door was shut and —"

The Rio Kid, gun in hand, was already running lightly across the stone-flagged *patio* toward Barron's room. The Johnny Reb was wounded, helpless, and the Rio Kid's quick mind saw deadly danger to Barron in such a thing as Bigfoot had described. Of course, the intruder might be just a sneak thief, but —

He was at the window. The sash was standing open. Clicking his pistol to full cock under his thumb, he jumped through into the dark room.

"Madre de —"

The Rio Kid, crouched to one side, away

71

from the lighter rectangle of the open window, heard the startled, gasping curse from near where Barron was lying. The young Southerner's even breathing told he was still asleep.

The Rio Kid caught the rustle of leather, as the fellow on the other side of the room shifted, and the shaft of light glinted on steel.

"Drop it, hombre!" Bob Pryor snapped in Spanish.

CHAPTER VII
DANGEROUS START

The Rio Kid fired once, high, so that the bullet shattered in the outer wall. The quick flare of the burning powder showed him Gasca's dark features, the *vaquero's* gleaming, clenched teeth. Gasca had been at the chest of drawers, hunting what he could steal before doing his job. This had given the Rio Kid the moments needed to get over.

With a bound the Rio Kid reached Barron's cot. The wounded man startled to consciousness by the explosion of Pryor's gun, cried out, "What's that?" and tried to sit up.

Gasca was still on the other side of the room, a black shadow in the gloom. The bunk was between the Rio Kid and the *vaquero*. It was difficult to make out any details, but Pryor saw the shadow that was Gasca move swiftly toward Barron, and saw the glint of steel.

He cursed, for want of a little light. Suddenly what he wished for came, the flare of a big sulphur match at the other window. Bigfoot Wallace's large head was stuck in, and he held the match stick in one hand, his pistol in the other.

The flame made Pryor certain of Gasca's intentions, for the man had his knife raised high, about to plunge it into Barron's heart. Gasca was rattled. He was trying to repair his error and finish off Barron, but the crouched Rio Kid, close on him, lifted his thumb off his Colt hammer again.

Gasca shrieked and collapsed. Barron yelled in pain as the heavy body fell across him.

Bigfoot Wallace, nursing his match and grinning, came inside. He touched the flame to a candle wick and the illumination showed the Rio Kid, feet spread, smoking gun up, his left arm out to balance himself as he made his shot.

Gasca, with the long, sharp knife still clutched in his fingers, lay on Barron's legs. His fall had jolted the young man but Arthur Barron had not been hurt by the blade.

Wallace seized Gasca's shoulders and yanked him off Barron, rolling him over so he landed, a dead weight, flat on the floor.

"Nice shot," grunted Bigfoot. "Got him in

the nose."

In the yellow light, the Rio Kid examined his victim. The heavy slug had made a blotch of the *vaquero's* face, but Pryor recognized him as the man he had chided when Gasca had fired on the Navajos.

"Huh," he growled. "What in tarnation!"

"Tryin' to rob yuh," said Bigfoot, grinning at the stunned Barron, who was blinking and licking his lips.

"Of what?" Barron wanted to know.

"Shucks, he prob'ly figgered yuh're rich, like all Yankees," replied Bigfoot, picking up the makin's from the table and fixing himself a smoke.

The Rio Kid was not sure. He wondered why Gasca, instead of trying to fight his way out, had gone for Barron that way, first of all. A quick search of Gasca's pockets yielded nothing, save some money and personal effects. He had a gun hidden under his leather jacket.

Nor could Don Francisco, roused from sleep by the shots, shed any more light on Gasca's actions. He was amazed at what Wallace and Pryor had to tell him. The *hacienda,* awakened by the rumpus, was astounded at Gasca's perfidy in attempting to rob and kill the young *Americano.* Yet none could say why Gasca should have suddenly gone to the bad.

There were armed guards outside. The fine saddled horse was found, with Gasca's pack on it, a pack containing food and outfitting for a long journey. They figured that he had meant to finish with Barron, then ride away.

Jed Hannigan, the editor and storekeeper, was among the crowd which collected.

"The dirty dog," Hannigan cried, as he learned what had occurred. "He only got what he deserved!"

"How long has Gasca worked for yuh, Don Perez?" inquired the Rio Kid.

"Six months, perhaps."

"Where'd he come from?"

"I think he worked for the Circle S before," Perez replied.

"This makes twice that Gasca horned in," mused the Rio Kid.

Before he had believed that the shot, fired by Gasca, which had precipitated the battle with the Navajos, had been a matter of a hot head and a hasty trigger finger. Now he was not so sure. Now Gasca was dead. He could not be questioned, and the mystery could not be cleared up at present.

After an hour, the people in the *hacienda* returned to bed, and the Rio Kid slept till the first gray streaks of dawn touched the sky.

He was up, then, hunting breakfast. Kit Carson, calm and sure of himself, was on hand, and after their hot meal, the two saddled up and said *adios.*

Mireles did not argue, but he watched the Rio Kid depart with tragedy in his dark eyes. He was never happy unless he was with his "General," as he insisted on calling Pryor, and the ticklish nature of the long trip Carson and the Rio Kid were making did not reassure him.

Bigfoot Wallace sang out hearty farewells, and the others watched the two riders leave the town and hit the road for the mountains. . . .

One who was left behind, however, was burning with an inner fury which he had a difficult time in concealing. That was Jed Hannigan. But somehow he forced himself to smile upon Don Francisco and the men of Valcito, though rage flamed in his black heart. Gasca, the fool, had failed him — and he had no other agent on hand that he dared entrust with the mission of contacting Egghead Pete.

"I'll have to go myself," he decided.

According to Hannigan's plans, Gasca should have been miles out, on his way, by this time, leaving Barron dead behind him. There was no time to bother with Barron now. Hannigan would be lucky if he could beat Kit Carson and the Rio Kid to Skeleton Peak, to signal Egghead Pete.

"That jackass Gasca must have thought Barron had some money," Hannigan thought, irritatedly, as he consumed a hasty breakfast. "He was always a hog for whatever he could squeeze out of a job."

On the plea that he wished to hurry back and check up on the stores needed by the Valcito men for the expedition against the Navajos, Hannigan took his leave only an hour after Carson and the Rio Kid had ridden away.

When he was out of sight of Valcito, he swung to a narrow trail leading to the mountains. His vicious eyes were always moving, right to left, ahead. His flesh crawled as he thought of what would be done to him if hostile Indians caught him, a white, out here. But desperation and his greed drove him on.

He kept looking for fresh sign of the passage of Kit Carson and the Rio Kid, for he must not run upon them. But he could see not the slightest track that told him they had come this way, and he kept pushing through the rocky, bushed trail, aware that every turn in it might mean a sudden, fatal ambush, the quick shot, the brutal leap of the savages and then torture until he died.

Hannigan did not reach the base of Skeleton Peak, a huge, grayish-white pinnacle that stuck up toward the blue sky, until after noon. In all the miles he had ridden the twisting deer trails he had not run on the least clue as to the course taken by Kit Carson and the Rio Kid.

Swiftly he gathered oily piñon knots together, and built a little fire, letting the smoke drift into the sky, on the west flank. Then he retired to some pine woods on a mountain slope, half a mile away, hid his horse and lay down to watch. In case the smoke attracted enemies, he would not be close enough to be caught.

His eyes burned with the intensity of his vigil, as hour after hour passed and there was no signal to show that Egghead Pete was coming. He cursed and stormed, but that did not bring the breed.

He was forced to replenish the fire twice during the afternoon. The sun was a huge crimson globe behind the western mountains at his rear before he saw a bronzed horseman spur a fleet little Indian paint pony across the rocky ground close to the smoke, and swing off around the bluff. He recognized Egghead's mount, and knew the rider was his agent.

Swearing a blue streak, but greatly relieved that his ordeal was at an end, Hannigan jumped up, seized his horse's reins, and led the animal down the steep slope until he could mount and ride over to the signal fire.

"Pete!" he called.

Egghead Pete, on foot now, peeked around a big rock not more than six feet from where Hannigan was standing. His nearness made Hannigan start with alarm.

"Come out here and quit playin' hide-and-seek," snarled Hannigan.

Egghead Pete stepped forth and joined him. Hannigan stared at him. Pete had changed somewhat. There was a queer air about him.

Two bloody scalps, one of a white woman who had long golden hair, hung at his belt. His torso was naked, showing old scars. His coarse black locks were bound with a white head-band, which had dark-brown stains on it, no doubt blood from his victims. Egghead Pete's shoe-black eyes were not dull now. They danced with red lights and were wide, as wide as such slits could be, and the pupils were dilated.

"Stop that noise," ordered Hannigan. He felt afraid.

Egghead was drawing in his leathery cheeks, then opening his lips. It sounded as though he were enjoying a piece of hard candy or warming up a chew of tobacco, but he was doing neither. It was merely the expression of the exaltation of his mood, for he loved killing, the warpath. Now and then he would gobble, an Indian's killing sound.

Hannigan knew that Egghead had the vindictive hatred for whites characteristic of many Apaches, who preferred to go down fighting rather than fall in with the new fashions, where Indians lived at peace with one another and their conquerors. He felt fear of Pete, for Egghead's manner was strange. But the breed made no hostile move toward him. He listened, nodding, as Hannigan began to talk.

"Where have yuh been, cuss yuh?" Hannigan said, with a bravado he was far from feeling. "I've waited here all day."

"We raid," grunted Egghead. "Good hunt." He patted the horrible tokens at his belt.

Hannigan didn't look at them. He was responsible for their being there, but he had distaste for such work. He could stand a man being shot, to lay where he fell. He did not change much in appearance, and someone else could bury him. Scalps were a dif-

81

ferent story.

"Kit Carson and the man we call the Rio Kid are on their way to the Navajos' mountain camp!"

Egghead Pete cursed them. He scowled, grimacing, his white blood coming to the fore as he was startled by Hannigan's news.

"Yuh didn't see 'em?" asked Hannigan.

Pete shook his misshapen head. "No see. Fader Kit too smart. No good. He talk too much."

"Yuh got any men with yuh?"

"Sure, sure. Ten. Good."

He shrugged toward the upper rocks. Up there, Hannigan knew, Egghead's renegades were hidden, no doubt with rifles trained on him.

"Hurry, then. Gasca was killed — the Rio Kid shot him last night, savvy? Catch up with 'em if yuh can and kill 'em both. If yuh don't beat 'em in, don't let 'em get back home. And I'll make shore that any Navajos who try to come out to talk to Perez won't do it. Ole can tend to that. Get goin' now and ride day and night. I'm on my way home and I'll see Stensen."

Egghead stared at him for a moment without moving. Then he nodded, turned, and evaporated as he swung silently around the rock. Hannigan did not see him or his men again although he kept looking around as he mounted and rode off seeking to make as many miles toward the main trail as possible before it grew entirely dark.

CHAPTER VIII
HOSTILES

Even though the Rio Kid was as skillful a scout as ever rode the dangerous trails of the West, he followed Kit Carson's lead, for the trip to the camp of the hostiles was Carson's party.

"I can guess just about where they've headed to," Kit remarked. "I've been all through here and savvy the country, and I think we'll foller Devil's Crik."

"Anything yuh say," agreed Pryor.

He had only the deepest admiration for the slender man who was a great scout. Kit Carson was a name to conjure with. Famous men were familiar with him and called on him whenever they had need of his genius.

Though sixty, Carson was still wiry, still able to outride, outthink and outwit any enemy.

Kit Carson did not take the direct trail, which led past Skeleton Peak. He veered some miles to the right, westward, after they had left Valcito behind. By training, by caution ingrained through a lifetime of moving through hostile country, where any instant might bring him face to face with death, Carson avoided leaving any sign, or covered it with a swift, unerring skill.

Ably assisted by the Rio Kid, Carson moved with precision. He lost no time and not much in mileage, although in order to keep hidden from distant spying eyes that possibly might be watching, he sometimes detoured to take advantage of a screen of trees, brush, or a long ridge running their way.

Both men kept their eyes moving unceasingly, from right to left, searching the ground they were passing, the sky.

Now and then, Carson would swing up from the lower sections, and take to a ridge, from which they could see the country for miles.

On one of these occasions, the Rio Kid pointed to the east. A far-off spire of grayish rock stuck up toward the heavens.

"Smoke over there, Kit."

Carson nodded. "I seen it. Skeleton Peak."

"Wonder what it means?"

Kit Carson shook his head. "It would take us half a day to work back and over to it, Rio Kid. Our first duty is to reach the

Navajos before all Hades breaks loose."

The Rio Kid pondered this. "Yuh reckon it may be worse than it looks?"

"Yes. A lot worse."

Carson did not elaborate. Always he was a man of few words, speaking only when necessary. There was no time for careless conversation, either, for the two men needed all their faculties for their journey, since they did not wish to tangle with any raiding Indian bands. That might mean a fight which would injure their chances with the Navajos.

Kit had an astounding memory for geographical locations. He needed no maps. His long experience in exploring untracked wilderness had endowed him with this faculty. The same experience had also made him a great rider.

Only once during the long day's run did Kit Carson deem it necessary to pause for any length of time. He came on a couple of burned sticks, and dismounted to examine them.

After a few minutes he straightened up. "We have nothin' to fear from this, Rio Kid," he said. "A Navajo hunter stopped here three days ago at dawn to cook himself a meal of deer meat. He's a hostile, but he's been a reservation Indian."

From a few signs invisible to most eyes, Carson had read exactly what had occurred days before. The Rio Kid, an able tracker himself, also could check the deductions.

They camped at dark, ate a cold meal, and slept, hidden in dense chaparral, their horses staked some distance away.

Before dawn they were up, had eaten and drunk, and were on their way again, toward the inaccessible mountain retreat where Kit Carson was sure Wolfkiller, the Navajo leader, had his people.

The route became more difficult. They had to pass through deep, shadowed canyons, and climb great slides of volcanic rock. Around noon, they came on faint signs which told them that the Navajos had passed this way with their animals — a bit of sheep's wool on a thorn, the fresh scratch of a hoof on a stone.

"We'll take to the other side of the mountain," Carson ordered. "I don't want them to see us until we're in close."

With the cunning Kit in the lead, they circled the tremendous barrier. It occupied the afternoon, and sunset was near as Carson stopped and pointed toward a wall of brush.

"They're in there," he declared. "There's a hidden box canyon with fresh springs and good grass for their stock. The Navajos call it the 'Chest of the Serpents'. It's crawlin' with snakes."

On foot Kit Carson went down a steep slide, his horse following, slipping sideward to make it. Saber came behind the Rio Kid.

"Take off yore gun-belts, and hang 'em on yore saddlehorn," ordered Carson.

He removed his own visible weapons, and the Rio Kid, hesitating but an instant, followed suit. But Pryor did not like placing his weapons so far from his hands, but he had two hidden pistols under his shirt.

"Foller me, now," said Kit, "and whatever yuh do, don't fight unless I start first, savvy?"

"I savvy. Lead on."

Reins in one hand and with the other swinging free and empty, the two scouts took a faint trail that led to the canyon entrance.

There was a sudden whoop and heavily armed Navajos leaped up on both sides, covering them with cocked rifles. They wore war paint and feathers.

Kit Carson nodded to them calmly, and spoke in their own tongue. He knew French, Spanish, and many Indian dialects, and the Navajos were well-acquainted with Father Kit. The Rio Kid did exactly as Carson did.

When the Indians snatched his horse's reins, he made no objection.

"Otasco," Carson said, in Navajo, to a tall, grim-lipped savage, "take me to Wolfkiller. I must talk to him."

Otasco nodded. He gave an order and the two scouts were escorted through the brush wall which opened under the Navajo hands.

A large crowd of Indians, squaws and children, and more armed braves, waited inside the gate.

The Chest of the Serpents spread out. Long grass covered the canyon bottom, and there were green spots where springs bubbled up from white sands. Beyond were the sheep and cattle and mustangs of the Navajos, driven up here for safe-keeping. Rough hogans of brush and hide had been thrown up for shelter, and gear lay about, as did gay-colored blankets and urns, weapons and clothing.

Up the trail stood a tall, majestic Navajo, wearing leather and a headdress of red, and eagle feathers.

Kit Carson walked easily toward him, his face grave but friendly, and held out his hand in greeting.

"Wolfkiller, my son," he said.

Wolfkiller, the local Navajo chief, had a stern face, long with high cheekbones. The sun of fifty winters had blackened his hide, and deep creases were in his forehead and about his grim lips. He wore a cartridge belt and a revolver, as well as the usual knife. Beautifully beaded moccasins, with uppers reaching to the knees, covered his feet. His bronzed arms were heavily muscled, ringed by beaten copper bracelets studded with turquoises.

"Father Kit!" Wolfkiller grunted.

Probably no white man save Kit Carson could have walked into Wolfkiller's presence at that moment. Anyone else would have been killed or tortured before entering the canyon, but they knew Kit. They loved and trusted him, for he had always been the Indians' friend.

"What madness is this, Wolfkiller?" Carson asked in the Navajo tongue. "I thought you and the people were too clever to make war on the whites."

"Huh!" said Wolfkiller, his lip curling disdainfully. "It is they who have gone mad, Father Kit. We will defend ourselves to the end, and so will our brothers, the Apaches."

To one side stood a tall fierce-eyed, proud Indian with a high forehead. He wore a white head-band about his inky locks, and his power was plain.

"Victorio!" thought the Rio Kid, with a shock.

Victorio, chief of the Warm Springs Apaches, was an important personage. He controlled hundreds of the best fighting men the world had ever seen, ruthless red raiders whose guerrilla tactics had so far baffled every general in the Army.

The Rio Kid had met Victorio on a previous occasion, during a fight in Arizona, and he realized what the famous Apache's presence here must mean. At the same moment, he comprehended what Kit Carson had hinted at when he had said that the situation might be worse than it seemed. If Wolfkiller banded his Navajos together with the Apaches, the war would not be just a local uprising. It would sweep the whole Southwest, from Mexico to Colorado, through Arizona, and the great state of New Mexico.

Hundreds of white men would die, thousands on thousands of dollars in property would be destroyed. A major military campaign would have to be undertaken by General Sherman, in command of the Southwest.

By Indian telegraph, the Apaches had been called. Victorio, a fighting man in his prime had answered, no doubt riding a couple of hundred miles without leaving his horse's back.

Moreover the presence of Victorio meant that old Cochise who lurked in Arizona, who loathed and abhorred white men and was ever ready to strike at them, would take a hand.

"Why," inquired Kit Carson, "do you say the whites began it, Wolfkiller, when you know your braves attacked the Perez sons and killed one of them and some of their friends? And why were you riding in a war party toward Valcito? And why had you already sent your women and children to the Chest of the Serpents, if you didn't intend to go to war?"

"Those are all lies, made up by the whites who have deceived Father Kit just as they deceived the Navajos," declared Wolfkiller. "The fact is that the white men have decided to kill us all, except the children and women, whom they will enslave. They want our flocks and our ancient lands but they won't get them without a big fight."

"Who told you all this?" insisted Kit Carson. "I want to see the man who has been eating loco weed. Where is he?"

The Rio Kid was absorbed in watching the strange, barbaric array of the savages. They were heavily armed and angry, stirred up like a seething hive of infuriated bees.

The dark, high-boned faces, the fierce black eyes, and the colorful clothing, copper and turquoise ornaments, combined with the painted rocks and wild land to form a stunning picture.

Both Kit Carson and the Rio Kid knew the Indian nature. They were like children and believed such all-inclusive yarns, when they were properly presented, as that the white race had deliberately begun to wipe out the Navajos and their brethren. Unable to comprehend the complex nature of the pale-faced race which had invaded their hereditary domains, the Indians were inclined to seize upon simple explanations.

Carson knew that to laugh at them and push their ideas aside without refuting the arguments would only injure the Indians' dignity and would not stop the rising war sentiment. He was playing for big stakes, and was aware of it. Once the redmen started in full force there was no saying where the matter would end.

The Indians would lose many of their men, and the helpless and weak would suffer untold hardship. Small settlements, such as Valcito, would undoubtedly be attacked, prisoners killed or tortured, and property damaged.

"I will tell you who gave the Navajos

warning of the murderous plans the whites have made," replied Wolfkiller, his head proudly up. "It was the Man-Whose-Mother-Dropped-Him. He knows the pale-faces, having lived with them. He overheard them plotting to steal our sheep and cattle and horses and our range!"

"Where is this fool?" ordered Father Kit. "Let me talk to him."

CHAPTER IX
TELLING ARGUMENTS

Intently watching Wolfkiller, the clever Carson, and Victorio, who was disdainfully standing to one side with his bronzed, muscular arms folded, the Rio Kid suddenly was rudely knocked off balance. He nearly went down, but saved himself by a twist of his lithe body. He frowned at the man who had bumped into him from the rear, but he did not retaliate, since Kit Carson had warned him against violence unless Kit ordered it.

It was Egghead Pete, although the Rio Kid had never met the breed. The fellow's misshapen head told why the Indians, apt at naming men for their physical peculiarities, called him as they did. His ears stuck out straight, his eyes were slanted, and his mouth a small, level gash in his ugly face.

He wore doeskin leggings and moccasins, but his torso was naked. At his belt hung scalps, one a fair-haired white woman's.

Navajos would not touch a dead person and seldom took scalps but Pete was of Apache strain. He had a pistol in a supple new leather holster and a knife, with a good carbine slung over his back.

"Yes, I said it, and I say it again!" shouted Egghead Pete boldly.

He bristled up to Kit Carson, shooting out his neck while his black eyes glowed blood-red. He made noises with his leathery cheeks.

"Why listen to their lying tongues, Chief?" Pete said to Wolfkiller. "Let me take their scalps. They are our enemies. Kill them!"

Kit Carson's shrewd eyes were fixed on Egghead Pete's. They never swerved. Lashing himself into frothing fury, Egghead gobbled and sought to outstare Father Kit, but at last he dropped his glance, at the same time placing a hand on his knife.

Kit Carson knew what to do. His own hand suddenly flashed out and he slapped Egghead Pete in the mouth with all his force, driving the fellow's flesh into his teeth. Then, without paying further heed to Pete, Carson deliberately turned his back on him, and went on talking to Wolfkiller.

The Rio Kid got ready. He had two hidden pistols under his buckskin shirt and he would use them to save Carson if necessary.

The blow, given to drive the lies back into the breed's mouth, the contempt which Father Kit showed for Egghead, impressed the Indians tremendously. Anyway, Egghead Pete was not a Navajo. He was not really an Apache, either, but only a volunteer ally. Would he dare to strike back at Father Kit?

Carson's back was to Egghead Pete, and the Rio Kid knew that he might rip Father Kit with the sharp point. For an instant, everything hung on Carson's bluff. The Rio Kid was tensed to spring, to finish Pete if he could before the breed got Kit.

Blood trickled from Egghead's lacerated lip. The effrontery of it had stunned him, and he stood, back on his heels, mouth open.

Then he began to swear, in white man's language, but still Kit Carson paid no attention to him. Low murmurs ran through the assembled Indians, murmurs of amusement. The Man-Whose-Mother-Dropped-Him was talking instead of acting.

Unable to build up his nerve to the point of attacking Kit Carson, Egghead Pete turned on his heel and stalked away, out of the canyon. He had traveled night and day without pausing in order to beat Kit and Pryor in, only to lose his nerve at the crucial moment.

The Rio Kid breathed easier. His admiration for Kit Carson increased, if that were possible. Carson had sized up Egghead correctly and had known just what to do to lessen his influence with the Navajos.

"You see how brave that liar is," Carson went on to the Indian chief, with a shrug. "You'd do much better to listen to me, Wolfkiller. Have I ever lied to you? Haven't I always tried to help the people? My sons have Indian blood in their veins and I know what you want. There has been a mistake made, and the thing to do is for the Indians to talk it over with the whites before going further with this senseless war.

"Who will win? Not the Indians, who will lose their bravest men and much of their property. Not the whites, who will have their people killed and their homes burned. If Perez and the men from Valcito can't defeat you, then will come Redbeard, General Sherman, with hundreds, or thousands of trained soldiers."

"We will fight them," said Wolfkiller.

"Yes, you will fight them! They will bring up the big guns they call cannon. A dozen shells thrown into your canyon will kill you by the hundreds — women, children and animals alike. And all because you listen to lies told by a liar."

98

Wolfkiller did not reply for a time, turning over Father Kit's sensible advice in his keen mind. He was a child in many ways, in outlook on the world as a whole. He was unable to realize its scope and the inexorable trend of destiny which drove the restless white man, the greatest and most efficient killer ever to rove the earth, on and on to seize what he desired.

On the other hand, he was wise in his own way, and logical. He had fought against trained troops in his brash youth and knew what cannon could do.

His people trusted Carson, too. His first wife had been an Indian, and Father Kit had always been kind to all Indians. If they insisted on fighting, then he could fight like an unconquerable fiend. But if they laid down their arms, he would feed them, help them, intercede for them with the Government of the United States.

"Very well," Wolfkiller said finally. "I will talk with my chiefs, and if we decide to parley, I will send the word to you."

The Rio Kid had seen a miracle. Kit Carson, unarmed, alone, had ridden into the hostiles' camp, had talked them over, and won. If Wolfkiller were ready to negotiate it meant he would not go to war on Egghead Pete's say-so. He would first hear the testimony of the Perez men and their friends.

Both Pryor and Carson were now suspicious of Pete. Egghead's lies must have some deeply sinister purpose. The fact that both Perez and Wolfkiller claimed the other side had started the fight must be carefully examined, and what had really occurred must be sifted out from the various stories of dependable witnesses.

"When will you speak with Senor Perez and the other white chiefs?" asked Kit Carson, pressing his advantage.

"Four suns from now."

"Where? Will you come to Valcito?"

Wolfkiller shook his majestic head.

"They must come part way, Father Kit. Say to Skeleton Peak. It is easy to approach, for both parties."

"Very good. In four days we will meet you at Skeleton Peak, Wolfkiller, and end this senseless war."

Wolfkiller shook his head. "They attacked us, for no reason at all. They burned our village. Some of our braves were shot down, when they were hunting, and our scouts reported that the whites who had killed them came from Valcito. The tracks led straight there. We were afraid and sent our flocks and women to the mountains for safety. Then our braves started for the white

100

man's town. Even then we were not sure. But they fired on us."

"A traitor, a fool, did that," Carson declared. "He's dead now, that Gasca. This man, the Rio Kid, killed him, Leader."

Wolfkiller's stern eyes flicked for a moment to the face of the Rio Kid, and he grunted.

"Good."

"Ask him," the Rio Kid said to Kit, "if his braves attacked the Perez boys that day."

Wolfkiller, when this question was put to him, shook his head.

Water and jerked deer meat were offered Kit Carson. The two whites had a quick meal, which might have been in the way of celebration. For, as he had done on numerous occasions during his long and brilliant life on the Frontier, Carson had walked into the jaws of death and had come out alive, victorious.

Their horses were returned to them, and the two scouts began their return trip to Valcito.

A party of Navajos, Wolfkiller's trusted braves, escorted them from the canyon and for two miles on the home trail. Then the comrades rode on.

Kit Carson smiled at the Rio Kid's congratulations on his success. Pryor had been able to comprehend a good deal of the talk, the sign language part of it, at any rate, and some of the actual words. Kit Carson retailed to him the shades of meaning which he had missed. ⌒

"There's somethin' fishy about the whole business," Carson declared. "Wolfkiller is not a liar, and the Indians are honestly indignant, their feelin's are hurt. They are shore they didn't begin the fight. As a rule the Navajos prefer to live in peace, with their flocks. They won't fight unless they are certain they're in the right and set upon. They seldom go in for scalpin', as yuh know. Different from the Apaches. Yet Francisco Perez certainly wouldn't stir up the savages by wanton attacks."

"How about that Egghead devil?" asked the Rio Kid, as their horses jogged slowly along the rocky trail.

Kit Carson shrugged. "We'll have to dig out the truth about him sooner or later. That kind sometimes raises ructions just for the fun of it. But he couldn't have stirred up all this fuss by hisself. He's had help. Those Navajos from Wolfkiller's village, now, who reported they were fired on by Valcito whites — the trackers follered them to the town."

The Rio Kid turned it over in his clever

mind. There were many ramifications to the trouble. Where did Gasca come in? Who were the white men who had so cunningly enraged the Navajos? Who were the Indians who had attacked Manuel Perez and his friends the day that Pryor and his two companions had come upon them? These questions must be answered before the matter could be cleared up.

However, the big point had been won. Wolfkiller had agreed to come in under a truce to talk, and many matters could then be thrashed out.

By nature both scouts were cautious, and so they continued to be as they rode on, although the strain had left them since Carson's great victory at Wolfkiller's camp. Without firing a shot he had almost settled the war. He had brought off such coups before and was loved and honored for it.

Chapter X
The Way Home

Kit Carson rode ahead. Saber, the Rio Kid's mouse-colored dun, had such a bad temper with other horses as the Rio Kid had explained, that if he got close enough to the bay on which Carson was mounted, he might bite a chunk from its hide.

To soothe Saber, the Rio Kid lightly hummed an old Army tune. The words of the verse ran:

Said the Big Black Charger to the
    Little White Mare,
"The Sergeant claims yore feed bill
    really ain't fare."
Said the Little White Mare to the
    Big Black Charger,
"Yuh forget, kind suh, that our
    family's growin' larger."

Saber loved the tune and if he heard it whistled when he was within hearing, he would gallop to his master. It soothed him now, eased his worry at not being able to use his teeth.

Their weapons had been returned to Carson and the Rio Kid, along with their mounts. The Rio Kid felt a lot more comfortable with his carbine under his leg, and his Army Colts close to his quick hands.

"We'll camp by Dead Horse Spring and cook up that chunk of deer meat," Kit Carson announced cheerfully. "It will be safe enough now that Wolfkiller's pacified. We can shield our fire after dark and the smoke won't be seen."

"Good. We better hustle it up, though, if we want to make it by sundown."

They were able to pick up a little speed on a level stretch. Then ahead lay a series of jagged ridges they must cross before dropping down into the valley where lay Dead Horse Spring.

Four hours out of the Navajo camp in the Chest of the Serpents, many miles behind them now, they were afoot, leading their horses along a precarious rock walk atop a ridge. Loose shale was under them and while the animals could negotiate it, without weight on their backs, they couldn't make it with riders.

Kit Carson was ahead, his bay's reins in

one hand, and balancing himself with the other. A ten-foot drop to a ledge was on one side, and below that a steep slide, of eroded rock, from which grew stub piñons and spruce that somehow found a foothold. On the other flank was a sheer gray-rock wall, streaked with rusty layers.

The sun was to the left, on the same side as the drop. It was as red as blood, and blinding when one looked that way.

Something zipped in the air between Kit Carson and the Rio Kid, and the bay snorted and reared in fright.

"Thirty-thirty bullet!" the Rio Kid said.

"Take it easy," cautioned Kit Carson. "We can't hurry here."

Another bullet bit a chunk from the Rio Kid's hat, and flattened itself against the rock wall.

Pryor could see the smoke puff from that one. It came from the opposing wooded slope of the ravine. As he followed after Kit Carson, balancing on the narrow ledge and steadying Saber behind him, three quick puffs, followed by the rapping bullets on the graystone, showed that more than one enemy was after them.

The range was a quarter of a mile, and the shooting none too good.

"Indians," decided Kit Carson.

Their foes were down low, keeping hidden, with only their rifles sticking out. A volley came, half a dozen rifles cracking. The Rio Kid felt a splinter of rock cut his right leg. Saber snorted and jerked back his head. He had been spattered by stinging lead.

Carson's bay was frantic as he, too, felt the rain of tiny fragments. But Carson and the Rio Kid could not shoot without danger of crashing over the edge. It was less perilous to try to make the safety of the next drop where the bullets would not reach them.

"Bad shootin'," remarked Pryor.

Kit Carson had but a dozen yards to go before he would be at the end of the narrow ledge. Then he could mount and ride to the ridge and over, out of range. Neither scout flinched, but it was no use firing revolvers, and to stop and get out their carbines would be a foolish move.

They kept moving, and Carson was almost to the safety of the end when a dozen smoke-puffs showed from the wooded slope, and the Rio Kid heard the bullets shrieking like hail about his ears.

"More of 'em there now!" he thought instantly. "Wonder how many all told." The next moment he muttered, as Kit Carson stepped out onto the easier ground, "There! He's all right now, anyways."

At that instant, however, the big bay horse reared high into the air. A bullet had plunked into his barrel ribs, and entered his vitals. Kit Carson turned, as the horse plunged violently back over the ledge. The scout tried to let go his reins, by which he had been leading the bay, but was jerked from his scant footing and went on over the lip after the kicking, screaming bay.

In that instant, from comparative safety, horse and rider were instantly plunged into the deepest peril.

The Rio Kid shouted as he saw Kit Carson fly over the lip of the rock, and land heavily on the shale slide ten feet below. The bay hit an instant before Kit and stayed where he was for a moment. Then, twitching in death, he rolled over, his haunches striking hard on Carson's chest.

Driven into the loose rock by the weight of the bay, Carson lay as he had landed. The horse rolled on, then slid, gaining momentum, for two hundred yards down the steep slope, before bringing up against a huge nest of jagged boulders.

A shriek of triumph rang from the woods across the ravine.

"Kit!" the Rio Kid cried, kneeling on the

edge of the drop. "Yuh bad hurt?"

Carson did not reply. He lay still. The Rio Kid saw blood welling from his lax mouth. His eyes were shut.

Cursing, frantic, the Rio Kid led Saber the last few feet. He uncoiled his lariat and hooked it to his saddle-horn.

"Stand, Saber — stand firm!" he commanded, and went down the rope so fast his calloused hands were burned.

The enemy made a tactical error then that helped Pryor. They cut down, rounding the lower huge rocks with the idea of getting up and taking Kit Carson and his companion prisoner. That gave the Rio Kid a few precious minutes in which to save Carson.

He got his arm under Kit Carson's shoulders to lift him, and looped his lariat about his friend. Tying the noose securely under the armpits, he lifted Carson, who was light, and propped him as upright as possible against the rock wall. Then he shinnied up the rope, held taut by the trained Saber.

"Back, Saber!" he ordered, and the dun obediently pulled.

Carson was drawn slowly to a point where the Rio Kid could get a hold on him and drag him to the ledge. He shouldered Carson and carried him off the narrow path of the rock.

A whoop of disappointment sounded and a couple of slugs struck close to him but Bob Pryor moved coolly, unrattled. He laid Kit Carson over Saber's back and led the dun over the ridge, dropping down out of range, no longer in sight of those charging up the slope.

Mounting behind the limp figure, he started to ride.

As the excitement subsided, he found blood flowing from a burn in his cheek, and from cuts he had received from sharp rocks. Examining Kit Carson as well as possible under the circumstances, he did not see any bullet wounds, although one side of the older scout's head and the cheek were cut from the fall.

Carson was still knocked out. His breathing sounded rasping, and the Rio Kid thought his chest might have been crushed by the weight of the big bay rolling on him.

There was no time to stop for anything, though the blood was welling from Kit's lips, but not in any large quantity.

"I'd like to go back and have it out with them devils, Saber," the Rio Kid growled, glancing over one stalwart shoulder. "But Kit comes first."

Not only was he devoted to Kit Carson, but he knew that on the scout's life depended the outcome of the pending Navajo war. With Kit Carson dead, it would probably continue to its terrible end.

He made as rapid time as possible, with Saber carrying double weight. Lucky that Carson was not a heavy man.

For a mile he kept pushing on, and it grew close to nightfall. He was riding across a grassy slope, some three hundred yards up from the valley bottom when several horsemen, Indians in war paint and feathers, came spurting along the little creek and opened fire upon him. He had no doubt they were the same party which had ambushed Carson and him on the ledge.

He was at the same disadvantage as he had been at the first attack. The sun was in his eyes, and he was one against a number. Five showed at first, seeking to slow him down with their slugs, their whoops sounding shrill in the confined spaces between the hills. Several more came up as he swung getting out his short-barreled carbine and opening fire at a thousand yards.

He was furious at the tantalizing, cruel assailants. If they had killed Kit Carson —

They rode like mad centaurs, clinging with a hand and knee to the far side of their horses, oblivious to the dangerous ground over which they sped. One came in at full-tilt, shooting rapidly up at the Rio Kid, and the bullets kicked up the dirt several yards from the moving dun's hoofs.

"Steady, Saber," the Rio Kid murmured, and the intelligent warhorse gave him a firm base from which to fire, as he threw his carbine to shoulder, took aim and, allowing for movement and windage, squeezed the trigger.

The Indian went flying off his staggering mustang which was struck by the Rio Kid's carbine bullet. He was running as he landed, lithe as a wild panther. An instant later the Rio Kid got him and the man immediately following him, sending both crashing face-down in the creek.

Shrieks of rage sounded at this minor triumph. The redmen blasted at him with their rifles, but they did not approach too closely.

The Rio Kid moved on, as the sun disappeared behind the mountains, a glorious glow in the sky. Glancing back, his keen eyes picked out the leader of the attackers — and an electric shock ran through him.

"Why, it's that egg-headed breed!" he growled. "So that's his game!"

He topped a rise, and dropped behind it, but did not ride far. Instead, he left the dun, with Carson still unconscious over Saber's back, beside a great boulder as a shield. On foot, with carbine in his hand, he ran lightly back to the ridge.

Chapter XI
Running Fight

Lickety-split the gang was riding up the slope. The Rio Kid let them get within five hundred yards before opening fire.

The vicious bark of his carbine then threw them into a panic. He hit the brave in the lead, and tried for Egghead, but the renegade was in the rear and the horse of one of his companions got it instead. They split up, veering off to the flanks, and wildly replying to his fire. He hit another in the ribs, knocking him from his horse. The rest ducked behind their mustangs and took out for cover.

Bob Pryor was down out of their sight again in moments, hurrying to the dun. But he knew they would not ride so brashly up on his tail again.

He made several hundred yards before he glanced back and saw them peeking over the ridge. But something more important took the Rio Kid's attention, as Kit Carson grunted and moaned feebly. He wasn't dead yet!

As speedily as he could, the Rio Kid cut down into a deep, heavily wooded valley, through which the dun picked a torturous trail. His foes kept doggedly on his tracks and night was almost at hand now. He was forced westward, off the way he knew that he and Kit Carson had come in.

He crossed the stream again and kept pushing ahead. And abruptly night fell, with the effect of a velvet blanket dropping on them.

Slowing, he listened. Behind he could hear crackling sounds. His pursuers were still coming on.

But they were no longer able to see him and tracking meant stopping, making a light, studying what faint signs the dun's hoofs might leave. He dodged like a fox, in and out, almost doubling back on himself. When at last he paused, he no longer heard them.

Kit Carson was grunting with every jolt of the horse. He needed attention, and as soon as the Rio Kid could stop he lifted him to a blanket he had spread out in a thicket. With his guns close at hand, loaded and ready, he sought to ease the old scout's pain.

He dared not light any fire, though the

dark had brought a coolness that made Kit Carson shiver. The Rio Kid covered him with everything he had, and gave him water to drink.

"How bad is it, Kit?" he whispered.

Overhead brilliant stars twinkled. There was a slice of moon rising over Skeleton Peak, many miles away.

"It's hard — to breathe," Carson told him painfully. "I dunno whether my chest is busted or not. Mebbe a rib or two."

"Lie still, then. Yuh got to rest for a while. Try to sleep."

Kit Carson shut his eyes. The Rio Kid, seated close to Carson's head, clasped his arms around his knees and sought to rest. He was worn out but he did not fully sleep, for he had to stay alert. Such trailers as Egghead Pete and his renegades could find a needle in a haystack even in the dark.

Kit Carson, however, managed to sleep. Three hours later the Rio Kid roused him, picked him up and set him on Saber, and started off again. The horse had had to have rest, and now that the Rio Kid knew that Carson was not in immediate danger of dying, the bleeding having stopped, he had to move on.

He was seeking a way in country of which he had little knowledge, in the night. Hitting a winding trail, and steering by the stars, the Rio Kid rode slowly, his carbine held in one hand, and the painfully grunting Carson held before him.

He had made no more than a mile back in the direction he knew Valcito must lie, when a dark figure leaped up before him and fired almost in his face. The flash was blinding. The carbine snarled like an echo. The Rio Kid felt the burn of lead in his hair, and the dun snorted and reared.

"Back — back!" gasped Kit Carson, startled to life.

The Rio Kid swung the horse in the constricted trail and drove off in retreat. His enemies were coming in, whooping in the darkness.

"Got — the trails all covered — that way!" Carson whispered hoarsely. "West — only way, Rio Kid — go 'round —"

Carson was right. Egghead Pete was blocking him off in the direction he knew that the Rio Kid would try to take.

It was slow going, the route the Rio Kid did take. The slope was steep, and through patches of spruce, pine and piñons. A touch of the gray of morning was in the sky when Saber wearily breasted the next divide.

The Rio Kid sought a doghole in which to spend the daylight hours. Saber must have rest, a chance to graze and drink, and Kit Carson kept fainting from the pain of the pace. A great thicket of spruce, black in the faint touch of the dawn, offered a haven. Pryor kept the dun on shale, until Saber could step onto the thick carpet of needles.

Fixing Carson as comfortably as possible, unsaddling the horse and tethering him where there was a patch of grass hidden in the trees, the Rio Kid crouched close to his friend.

"You — Rio Kid," whispered Carson. "Go on when yuh're rested — leave me. Yuh can bring help."

The Rio Kid shook his head. "Them red devils would come up with yuh, shore, Kit, 'fore I could get back. I won't leave yuh."

Carson closed his eyes again; he slept. For a time the Rio Kid dozed but every unusual sound brought him alert, gun rising.

Toward high noon he got up and climbed to the upper branches of a huge spruce. Far to east, the direction from which he had been driven in the darkness, he glimpsed a bronzed rider, slowly heading toward the woods.

Eventually they would guess where he and Carson were. He had, however, some time before they would be able to narrow it down.

Kit Carson was a bit stronger by dark. Cold food and water from the canteens, helped both men. Saddling the dun once more, the Rio Kid pushed on.

The inexorable enemy never gave up. At dawn the following day, a pair of big Indians — two of Egghead Pete's followers — almost stepped on the Rio Kid. One had a revolver in hand, the other a rifle. Both had long knives and white men's scalps at their belts.

Pryor shot the leader in the chest, killing him. The second fired a shot that was buried into the sand between Carson and the Rio Kid. Then he turned and dropped, rolling into the brush and rocks. He escaped the avenging bullets of the Rio Kid, and his shrill signals rang across the wastelands.

"We'd better get goin', Rio Kid," Carson grunted. "Help me up."

He was not suffering as much, but was still in pain. He knew the trails and directed the way, but Egghead Pete was again aware of their location, and the cat-and-mouse game continued. They were forced many miles into the wilderness, off their course.

The Rio Kid was determined not to lose Kit Carson. Too much depended on the great scout — the settlement of the threatened war, and the pride of the Rio Kid. . . .

■ ■ ■ ■

As days and nights passed in this running
fight in the wilderness, the same days and
nights had done much to put another man
— Arthur Barron — on the road to recovery.

Back in the Perez *hacienda* in Valcito, on a
bright morning, young Art Barron stretched
his powerful limbs in youthful pleasure. He
felt stronger and almost well, after the
ordeal through which he had gone. His
wounds had healed rapidly and the shock
from the brain concussion had worn off.

It was a week since he had been attacked
in his night camp and his horses run off.

From his chair in the sunshine of the *patio*
he could see the busy workers of the great
hacienda. Don Francisco had piled big
stores of ammunition and other necessary
articles, sent over from Hannigan's, in one
corner.

But there was one special person for
whom Barron kept watching. She had
helped to nurse him through his trouble,
and he found himself thinking more and
more of Senorita Dolores, the young daughter of the house. She had smiled on him,
and although they had never been alone
together, for her mother or a *duenna* had

always been at hand, Barron had secret hopes that she didn't find him uninteresting.

Manuel Perez who was about the same size as Barron, had loaned the young Southerner some clothing — velvet trousers that clung to the legs, a silk shirt, and handsome knee boots. These fine garments eminently fitted Barron's lean figure.

He liked the *hacienda* and the pleasant life here. These people were sociable, kind, and full of graces. An added tie was that good horseflesh meant as much to the Perez men as it did to Barron.

Finally Dolores appeared with her mother. With them was a woman servant who carried a laden tray, containing Barron's dinner. The ladies remained with him while he ate, heartily. The food was well-cooked, excellent.

Only with their eyes could Barron and Dolores speak what such young people might feel toward one another. Their words were formal but even so had such meaning. And when Dolores left Barron, somehow the morning was no longer so bright.

That evening, Bigfoot Wallace, the giant in buckskin who was the Rio Kid's friend, sauntered in and squatted beside Barron, who was in his room, with a lamp burning on his table.

"I just can't set on a chair or a bed," lamented Bigfoot. "I got into my habits young, Barron, and it ain't easy to change."

Barron smiled. He liked the huge frontiersman. Celestino Mireles, the tall young Mexican who always before had been the Rio Kid's trail mate appeared at the open *patio* door and slouched there, a cigarette trailing smoke from his lean brown fingers. He was restless, and his deep-sunken, dark eyes glowed in his sharp face.

"It's four days since Kit and the Rio Kid left for Wolfkiller's camp," complained Wallace. "I'm sick of hangin' round here, Barron, with nothin' to do but eat and say, '*Si-si.*' Besides, it's too full of women, and they upset me."

"You're not thinking of trying to follow Carson and Pryor, are you?" asked Barron.

"Nope. It might make real trouble for 'em even if they ain't already in it. By this time their ha'r may be danglin' from some redskin's belt."

Bigfoot shrugged, glancing around to wink at Mireles, who did not like that sort of talk.

"I reckon on allowin' 'em at least a week," continued Bigfoot, " 'fore I go on the warpath. Howsomever, there's no reason why I should hang up here. I want yuh to tell me just where yuh lost yore hosses that night. The Rio Kid said he was interested in that, and it'll be somethin' to occupy my time. Mireles feels the same way. He don't want to go far, 'cause Pryor may show up any time, but we got to have somethin' to do."

"I could show you the spot, if I could ride," Barron replied. "Not knowin' the country, though, makes it hard to tell you, without backtracking."

"How soon yuh figger yuh can fork a hoss?"

"Maybe tomorrow. I feel fine. I'll try it in the mornin'."

Next day he found he was able to sit the saddle of the black horse Manuel willingly had saddled for him. The motion hardly jolted his healing wounds, and he was delighted to be out in the open again.

With Bigfoot Wallace and Celestino Mireles, Barron started on the trail, seeking the spot where he had been ambushed.

Before noon, after three hours' riding, they came to the spot in the mountain trail where Barron had camped. It gave him a psychological shock to see it, for it brought back the anguish and the startling sensations of the attack.

"Sign's mighty cold," grumbled Wallace

as, on hands and knees, he began casting about, sniffing like a big dog. "These are yore boot tracks, Barron — and say, here's another heel mark. Yuh figger Injuns done it! Mebbe so. One might've kilt a white man and stole his boots."

CHAPTER XII
STOLEN HORSES

Bigfoot would not allow Barron and Mireles to approach too closely as he examined the spot. For about an hour he swore and talked to himself, touching the tracks, getting his eyes close to them. He was eking out every clue, and familiarizing himself with individual marks left behind by horses and men.

"C'mon," he said at last.

He mounted and led the way, back down the slope, toward Bubbling Springs, the valley settlement where Jed Hannigan had his store. His eyes were always on the trail. Now and then he would shake his head and curse.

When they had ridden nearly down to the level, he stopped altogether and left his horse. There he cast up and down both sides of the road like a hound that has lost a scent.

"Huh!" he cried, after twenty minutes of this. "They hid it good but they can't fool Bigfoot Wallace. Let's go, boys."

He shoved his horse into the brush, and rode a zigzag course, until even Barron could, in a soft spot, see the marks of many hoofs crossing. Down a wooded slope they went, and over the creek. In the clay showed the hoof marks.

Three miles further on, with the smoke of the town showing in the distance to their right, Bigfoot drew up in a patch of spruce on a low hill.

"Lookit the ranch down there," he remarked.

On the flat, set by a bend in the creek, lay a ranch. There was a rough house made of pine logs, with a dirt and brush roof, several sheds and a barn of native timber. Corrals, with cattle and horses in them, could be seen at the rear. Some barbed wire fence was strung here and there.

"Let's lie doggo for a while," ordered Bigfoot, "and see what happens. 'Course yore hosses may not be there, Barron, but the tracks p'int to it."

For a time they watched the ranch from their place of concealment. They saw only one man, a bowlegged fellow in cowboy garb, who came out of the big barn and went into the low-roofed house.

"They're out, workin' the range," concluded Bigfoot. "C'mon, boys, we'll take a look-see down there. That trail leads in to the corrals, far as I can make out."

"Hadn't we better get help — a sheriff or someone?" suggested Barron.

"I'm help enough in myself, ain't I?" replied Bigfoot, in a huff.

Barron said no more but followed Wallace and Mireles at a smart clip right up to the front porch. There was a circle with an S enclosed in it nailed over the door.

"Hey, in there!" sang out Bigfoot.

The bowlegged wrangler came dashing out the door and brought up short, staring at them, his chin dropping. He had tow hair and seamed, rheumy blue eyes, washed-out from the sunlight. He needed a shave badly. There were guns in his holsters, but he made no attempt to go for them when he saw the visitors.

"Wh-wh-what th-the —" he sputtered.

"Oh, yuh're durn s'prised to see us?" said Wallace, pleased. "Where's the boss?"

"H-he ain't h-home!" said the wrangler sullenly. "I — yi — I'm a-alone."

"That's a s-s-s-shame. Well, we're here to keep yuh company. Let's all go over to the barn and look at the hosses. Ours get lonesome, too, and if yuh got any they'd love to meet 'em."

Bigfoot had drawn his heavy pistol and

was fondling it, and Bowlegs obediently hurried across the side yard to the stable.

They dismounted, dropped their reins, and stepped through the wide doors. Stalls were at both sides, and at what Art Barron saw in them he gave a cry of joy.

"They're here! Those are my horses, boys!"

The dozen fine animals he had brought from Kentucky were in the stalls. One of them that had been something of a pet whinnied a greeting to the young man.

Bigfoot was triumphant. "We'll run 'em out and over to Valcito 'fore the thieves get back. I —"

"Look out!" Mireles cried.

He whipped out his pistol and fired a hasty shot from the open doorway, leaping back. Bigfoot Wallace jumped to the opening, cursed furiously as a slug bit a chunk of hide from his bearded cheek. Bowlegs gave a shrill yip and dived into a stall, while Barron, following Wallace up front, drew his gun and more cautiously peeked out.

A number of men, a dozen at least, had come stealthily from the ranchhouse, armed with rifles and Colts, and were edging into a circle about the barn. As Celestino gave the alarm, they had pulled their triggers and the bullets had driven through the boards.

One of them, Barron saw, was the big man who had fought him in the nearby settlement the day the Rio Kid had interceded for him.

Bigfoot Wallace, kneeling by the opening up front, took careful aim and shot again. He gave a curse of satisfaction as someone outside began yelling with pain. He had made a hit. Mireles, cool in a fight, let go with his gun. The men outside ducked for cover, and the three saddled horses, a short distance from the barn door, stampeded with panic as bullets hummed about their ears.

"Where's that bowlegged rat!" snarled Bigfoot, between shots. "Imagine me bein' fool enough to believe him when he said there was nobody home!"

Bowlegs had disappeared. There was a small window in the stall into which he had run and no doubt he had slipped through it.

A gun roared in the rear, and the slug narrowly missed killing Barron, squatted near Wallace.

"Take the back flank, there, Mex," Bigfoot ordered. "I'll cover the front. Barron, yuh better rove from one side to the other, savvy? Hug up close to one wall and yuh can sorta watch both."

Wallace's overconfidence had placed them in a ticklish position. The giant frontiersman was not the sort of man to hesitate over putting his neck into a dangerous situation. He was utterly without fear and had come through the most amazing adventures without getting fatally punctured.

He had been one of the hundred and seventy Americans in the ill-fated Mier expedition into Mexico, all of whom had been captured when their ammunition had run out. Black beans had been mixed with white beans to the same number as there were men in the party and every tenth soldier who had drawn a black one had been executed. But Bigfoot had escaped.

Indian arrows, bullets galore, had failed to check his career. Naturally he had figured that the house would be empty in mid-afternoon. Instead, it was full of angry, armed devils.

The barn walls did not stop the lead flung at them. They only made it difficult for the attackers to see the three inside. Where there were posts, thick enough to hold the driving slugs, were the sole spots where it was safe for the defenders to pause.

Barron crouched in a stall under a half-window, and peeked through a crack in the board sides. He glimpsed the big Stensen, evidently the chief of the gunnies about the ranch, and tried for him, but Stensen ducked behind the wagon he was using for cover.

"We'll wait till dark, boys," Bigfoot Wallace announced grimly. "Then we will grab us hosses and ride for it."

Jed Hannigan was hastily preparing the weekly issue of his little Frontier newspaper, the *Gazette*. It had four small pages, and he was writing scare headlines.

NAVAJOS RAGE ON THE WARPATH
WOLFKILLER'S RED DEVILS
SLAY WHITE WOMAN AT
THREE SPRINGS

He was playing up the war. He chuckled as he read another front-page item he had made up.

KIT CARSON MISSING
BELIEVED DEAD

Christopher Carson, Indian agent at Taos, is thought to have been slain by the Navajos whom he tried to help. Foolishly venturing into the heart of the hostile country, Carson made an effort to talk reason to a pack of savage beasts who repaid him by ambushing him on his way out. His horse was found by a sheepherder who reported it had been shot and had fallen over a cliff.

Carson was accompanied by the Rio Kid, a Texas gunman known in the Lone Star State as a quick-draw artist. The Rio Kid shot up our town one day but Fate has caught up with him. Perhaps even Wolfkiller didn't want to deal with such a man whose hands are stained with the blood of many victims.

The loss of Kit Carson will be felt by all who knew the old scout.

Hannigan let himself go on the Rio Kid, who had caused him so much trouble. He was sure, from what Egghead's messenger had reported, that both Carson and Pryor would be run down and slain in the wilds.

All was working out perfectly, according to his plans. After seeing Egghead Pete at Skeleton Peak, Hannigan had ridden home.

Egghead Pete's Indian aide had come to him, telling that Carson and the Rio Kid had reached Wolfkiller by roundabout trails and had mollified the Navajos. In four suns Wolfkiller and a dozen of his chiefs were to be at Skeleton Peak to meet the whites from

Valcito, under a truce to settle the war issue.

He also reported that Kit Carson was seriously hurt, and that Egghead was driving the Rio Kid and the agent into the wilderness to kill them. They would not escape.

Hannigan had once called in Ole Stensen. With his white cowboys, Stensen had ridden full-speed for Skeleton Peak and set his ambush there. The night before, Stensen had returned to say that they had opened fire on Wolfkiller and his Navajos, wounding the chief and several others. The Navajos had fled back into the mountains.

And now, late in the afternoon, he glanced up to see Bowlegs, one of Stensen's followers from the Circle S, throw himself from his horse and hurry inside the *Gazette* office.

"What's up, Bowlegs?" inquired Hannigan, taking the stogie from his wet lips.

"O-ole s-s-s-said to t-tell yuh h-he h-has Bar-ron and the-e M-mex and the b-big feller trapped in the-e b-b-barn!"

Hannigan jumped up. "Only the three of 'em? Yuh shore?"

Bowlegs nodded.

"I'll go out myself," said Hannigan, snatching up his gun-belt and coat and hat.

"I want to make certain they don't escape this time."

CHAPTER XIII
DISTINGUISHED VISITORS

Jogging along slowly, two scarecrow figures rode up the large public square of the old town of Taos.

One was the Rio Kid, but it was difficult to recognize the usually debonair, well-groomed rider in the clay-covered man in ripped clothing who topped the weary dun horse. Dried blood, from long thorn tears, showed on his face and arms, and a layer of dust had caked on his bearded cheeks.

He rode doggedly, teeth gritted. Kit Carson, hanging to his companion's waist, was only partly conscious. Saber, having carried double for many miles, in the roundabout run they had made to Taos, was utterly worn. Burrs matted his dark mane and tail, and on his hide were a couple of long creases that had come from bullet burns.

Kit Carson looked like a ghost. He had lost many pounds during the ordeal, as had the Rio Kid. The way to Valcito had been blocked to them by Egghead Pete and his renegades, and they had dodged like foxes before getting around and heading for Carson's home.

The straggling old settlement, with its houses of sun-baked adobes reminding the Rio Kid of so many brick-kilns, had narrow, crooked streets. In the center was a great plaza, as in all Spanish towns of the Southwest. Sheep, pigs and mongrel dogs rooted or basked in the sunlit dirt, while children ran shrieking and playing among them.

Kit Carson woke up long enough to mumble:

"That's my place over there."

The Rio Kid was suffering intensely. He was starved, and his eyes were burning, red, from lack of sleep. Dark shadows lined them, and his cheeks were gaunt. Still, he and Kit Carson had made it, and the ordeal was over. After days of running fight, he had eluded Egghead Pete's renegades and had reached Taos, with Kit Carson still alive.

Carson's home, though of but one story, was the largest and roomiest in Taos. It faced the plaza on the west side, spreading over a great extent of ground.

Everybody who went to Taos called on Father Kit, for he was affectionately called that by white men as well as Indians. And whenever the authorities had a delicate job to be done among the reds, they were sure to call on Kit Carson.

As the Rio Kid swung the worn dun to the wide gates of the *hacienda,* a brood of dark-haired children came galloping out, wild as young mustangs. There were half a dozen of them, Carson's offspring by his second wife, a Mexican woman of good family.

"Pop — Pop!" they began to shriek in Spanish. "Hey, Ma, Pop's come home. He's all dirty!"

Carson's wife hurried forth, crying out in excitement. She helped the Rio Kid lift Kit down and support him as he staggered to his bedroom.

Pryor walked unsteadily back, the world dancing before his eyes. He let Saber have a little water, rubbed him down, then turned him into a corral to rest and graze. There was a barn at hand and the Rio Kid went inside, seized a horse blanket from a peg, and threw himself down in the hay. . . .

It was night when the Rio Kid awoke. He was sore and his muscles were stiffened, but he felt refreshed, and hungry as a wolf.

The odor of cooking reached his widened nostrils. He went out and gave Saber more water, then repaired to the kitchen, where

Mrs. Carson was busy.

"How is Kit?" he inquired anxiously.

"He'll be all right," she replied. "His chest is hurt, though. He's got to rest. But he can eat and drink."

"*Bueno.*" A border man who spoke Spanish as easily as he did English, the Rio Kid always used that language with Spanish-speaking people.

Mrs. Carson set food before him — fried beef and potatoes, hot coffee, baked bread and molasses. The Rio Kid waded in, thinking he would never fill up.

The hot meal gave him new power. He had a smoke and, feeling much better, strolled in to see Kit.

Carson was sitting propped up in his bed. A man was in the room with him, a tall, lean fellow of nearly Carson's age. He had a sharp, intelligent face, and quick dark eyes which sized up Bob Pryor on the instant. There was an air of command about him, which the Rio Kid was quick to note, even as his eyes took in the man's curly dark hair, touched by gray, his beard that matched his locks, and his well-tailored Eastern clothing.

"This is the man I told you of, John," Kit Carson said. "Rio Kid, shake hands with John Frémont, my oldest friend."

"Howdy, suh." The Rio Kid smiled, sticking out his hand, which the other man seized.

Pryor had heard a great deal about Frémont, the famous explorer. He knew that the United States had John Charles Frémont chiefly to thank for the acquisition of California. His scientific surveys of the West and Southwest had made him a national hero.

But the Rio Kid knew more about him. He knew that however great Frémont had been as an explorer, with Kit Carson his guide, that he had not been so successful in political and military fields. The Rio Kid knew all about the man's defeat when he had run against James Buchanan in '56 for President of the United States, and how when he had been a major-general in the Civil War he had been court-martialed for acting too independently. His fortunes at the moment, the Rio Kid soon gathered, were at a rather low ebb, and he had stopped to visit his old comrade, Kit Carson, on his way through to Arizona on a mining expedition.

" 'Fore we talk," the Rio Kid said to Carson, "I wanted to ask if yuh'd sent word to Perez? I was so dogged tired when we got in I couldn't think of anything."

Kit Carson nodded. "Yes. I sent two messengers over to him, to tell him about Wolfkiller. But we've had a bad bit of luck, Rio Kid. We were too late, gettin' home."

"What yuh mean?"

Carson's face was sad. A few hours' nap and hot food had done wonders for him. His breathing was better, and while his chest still hurt him, the danger of immediate death had passed. But an even greater worry now seemed to obsess him.

"Of course Perez never knew Wolfkiller was to be at Skeleton Peak to talk peace," he said sadly. "Word came through yesterday that when the Navajo chiefs arrived at the Peak they were fired on from ambush by white men. Wolfkiller was wounded. They took to the chaparral — and that means real war now."

The Rio Kid cursed.

"They beat us, then, just holdin' us out that way! It's plain, Kit, there's some folks who're mighty hot on keepin' this war goin', ain't it?"

"I'd agree with that." Carson nodded.

"I'd like to know why. That egg-haided renegade must be workin' with 'em, and there are whites in it — the ones who fired on Wolfkiller and his Navajos. Egghaid got word to 'em one way or another, while he was keepin' us busy!"

"Yuh're right. It's mighty sad and it's serious. I have a wire here from General Sherman. It came to Santa Fé and was brought over by a Ute dispatch rider. Sherman's in charge of the Southwest and he's heard of the Navajo uprisin'. He's on his way here. I guess he'll light any time, and he wants me to scout for him."

The Rio Kid knew what that meant, and he understood Kit Carson's unhappiness. There would be little victories for the Indians, a few battles won. Their war trail would be marked by dead whites, and burned homes and ranches. But in the end the Indians would be the worst victims, for then Sherman and his trained troops would come and smash them.

"It's got to be cleared up," declared Pryor.

Frémont listened to the talk. "You ought to get word to this Perez and if possible to Wolfkiller, of what you suspect," he advised. "Have you any tame Indians you can send out, Kit?"

"Yes," answered Carson. "But whether the Navajos will believe anything, after what happened at Skeleton Peak, I don't know. However, perhaps Perez'll hold back if I ask him."

"I'll ride over to Valcito, first thing in the

mornin'," offered the Rio Kid, "and see what I can do, Kit."

"*Bueno.* I'll be there as soon as I'm able to ride." He turned to Frémont. "Mebbe you'd like to come along, General?"

Frémont nodded. "Be glad to, Kit. I've never been through that part of the country."

In spite of his recent long sleep, the Rio Kid again turned in shortly after. He slept until the first tinge of gray in the east. Then, a new man, he saddled up his dun after breakfast and headed for Valcito.

He arrived before noon. Armed men were thick in the town, and he trotted up to the Perez *hacienda* to find Don Francisco making ready to ride out at the head of his friends, to clash with the Indians.

"*Amigo mio!*" Don Francisco exclaimed, seizing the Rio Kid's hand. "I never expected to see you alive again! Word came that Senor Carson and you had been slain by the redskins! Then, last night the message from Carson, which I don't comprehend. I can't hold my men longer. Manuel started yesterday morning with fifty scouts to locate the Navajos, and I must follow."

"Kit hoped yuh'd hold off a little while longer," the Rio Kid said soberly. "There's somethin' fishy in the whole business, Don

142

Francisco."

He told the leader of their journey to the Navajo stronghold, of the interview with Wolfkiller, and how the Indians claimed the whites had begun the war. Then he described the running fight with Egghead.

"Was it yore men who fired on Wolfkiller when he came to Skeleton Peak?" he asked in conclusion.

Don Perez shook his head. "No. But it is all a mystery. Perhaps the Indians are lying. They are great ones at making up such stories. A band of them fired into the town again yesterday, and wounded one of my men. There is nothing to do but fight."

"General Sherman's comin' in."

Perez shrugged. "So much the better. When the troops come, they will be able to keep the Indians on a reservation. I can wait no longer to strike."

The Rio Kid, turning, strode into the *hacienda*. He wondered where Celestino was, for as a rule, Mireles would have been eagerly watching for him.

He did not see Bigfoot Wallace, either. And when he glanced in at Barron's room, he found it empty.

Just then a soft voice said:

"Senor Pryor! I am so happy to see you!"

Swinging, he found Dolores Perez at his

143

side. She had slipped away from her mother for a moment, and had hurried to speak to him. She was more beautiful and appealing than before, it seemed to the Rio Kid who already thought she was one of the finest girls he had ever met. Her dark eyes, as a rule filled with the joy of life and happiness, were now sad. She looked as though she had been crying.

"What's wrong?" he asked, staring down into her upturned face.

"They haven't come back," Dolores replied. "I am afraid."

"Who's that?"

"Senor Barron. And Celestino, and the man they call Beegfoot."

The Rio Kid started. This was the first he had heard of any expedition undertaken by his three friends. He had believed them to be somewhere near, perhaps out for a short ride.

"How long they been gone?" he asked quickly, when Dolores had explained how the trio had ridden off, to attempt to trail Barron's stolen horses.

"Since yesterday morning," she told him.

"Huh. They might've hit a long trail and camped overnight."

"Maybe. But — I am afraid. Will you go?"

"After 'em? Yes, I reckon I will."

In a short time the Rio Kid was on his way. He knew the tracks of the horses ridden by Bigfoot Wallace and Mireles. He did not know the tracks of the mount Arthur Barron had borrowed from the Perez stable because Greyboy was not yet in condition to be ridden far. Greyboy was out in pasture recovering from his injuries. But knowing the tracks of the other two mounts would be sufficient.

Bigfoot Wallace and the two with him had made no attempt to conceal their tracks, the Rio Kid discovered, and their trail was as easy for him to follow as though they had deliberately left a blazed way. He paused at the mountain niche where Barron had made his camp, and briefly examined the sign, realizing that here they had picked up the clues needed to stay on the course of the stolen horse band.

The sun was hot in an azure sky. A wind kicked up the red dust as he moved swiftly after his friends. In the distance colored peaks thrust their heads high. Reaching the point where Bigfoot and the others had cut off the road, the Rio Kid plunged into the brush and again had easy trailing.

So far there had been nothing alarming. They might, of course, have come up with the horse thieves and got themselves into

145

hot water. On the other hand the run might have proved too long to make in twenty-four hours.

CHAPTER XIV
THE FIGHT AT THE CIRCLE S

Mid-day had passed, when the Rio Kid sat his dun, on the hillside, looking down at Stensen's Circle S. Here his three partners had paused, just as he was doing. The place, which he did not as yet know was Stensen's, Hannigan's big friend with whom he had had the brush when defending Arthur Barron, looked peaceful in the shadowed light. It seemed to be deserted.

"I reckon they'll savvy if my pards went by," he decided. "They'd stop for a drink and directions, if nothin' else."

He could see no men about the house or the barn as he started the mouse-colored dun down the slope toward the ranch.

He had made but a hundred yards in the clear, headed downhill, when a bullet from the barn shrieked over his head. Then another struck wide, into the dirt.

Whirling the dun, the Rio Kid galloped along the hill and took cover, dismounting and staring down at the ranch.

"Pore shootin'," he thought. "Now what —"

Naturally he watched the barn, from which the shots had been directed at him. Suddenly he saw an object sail from a mow door, the opening into which hay was pitched on the second floor of the barn. It was a big sombrero, and as the person who had tossed it exposed himself an instant, three guns barked from various points about the barn.

"I savvy!" he growled. "They're treed!"

The Rio Kid's quick brain began functioning as he figured, with a trained military leader's skill, what to do.

"They been in there all night," he thought, remembering the swift trail he had followed. " 'Cause they would have got here 'fore sundown. Bigfoot would shore try to rush for it in the dark, but they must've been drove back in. On the other hand, those hombres who're holding 'em haven't enough force to overwhelm three such fighters. Wonder if I got time to fetch some help?"

But he shook his head. What would the enemy do in such circumstances? Why, when held off, they would get more help themselves, and as soon as possible. That

148

meant he must work fast.

"Can't be more'n a dozen or so holdin' 'em in," he decided. "They're waitin' for their pards to show up, I'll bet my hide on it."

He unshipped his carbine and made it ready, checked his Colts, his eyes taking in the terrain.

At the shooting several men had emerged from the front door of the ranchhouse, although they kept the building between themselves and the dangerous barn. Even at the distance the Rio Kid could make out the large size of one. He looked familiar.

From his saddle-bag, the Rio Kid extracted the small mirror he always carried. He made good use of it, too, trained as he was to neatness and to keeping himself well-groomed. Now it served another purpose. Catching it against the sun, he began to flash his orders to his friends in the barn. They would be watching through their peep-holes, since they knew he was there. Mireles had no doubt tossed out his hat to signal his comrade, and he had himself taught Celestino the code.

"Be ready!" he signaled.

A bullet from the men in front of the ranchhouse hunted for him in the brush. He threw his carbine to his shoulder, took careful aim, allowing for windage and distance. As the weapon barked, one of the fellows close to the big leader jumped and clapped his hand to his side. It was excellent shooting, and it threw a jolt into them, so that they hurriedly ran inside the house.

He heard a distant cheer from the barn.

He hated to run Saber straight onto guns, in daylight, to save the mount he had already made his plan of attack. A small creek ran through the valley in which the ranch stood. Scrub cottonwoods grew on its banks, and off to the right, as it entered the flats, the brush was thick.

He dropped back, and moved under cover to a point where he could reach the stream. Leaving Saber, he carried his rifle and pistols and ammunition belts, but discarded his spurred boots in favor of moccasins for easier running.

Hidden by the bank of the creek, the Rio Kid moved in on the Circle S.

The men there holding the Rio Kid's friends prisoners in the barn were rattled, nervous about him, and where he was. Men were watching from the house windows and from the points where they lay covering the barn. He paused, to peek cautiously through the brush. Now he could see two dead horses lying a few yards from the barn, and guessed they had died when his friends had tried to rush out.

He also saw a man with a rifle lying flat behind a small corn crib. He was holding that position to prevent the trio's escape.

At this angle, the big barn hid the Rio Kid from the house, where the chief force was concentrated, ready to rush into action if the captives tried to get away. On foot they would be run down, before they could make any distance.

He threw his carbine to his shoulder, took careful aim, and pulled trigger. He shot, not to kill, but to wound. The man stretched on the earth behind the crib was hit in the thigh, and flopped over, screaming bloody murder.

Leaving his carbine, the Rio Kid ducked down, and ran in the shallows of the cool water. Past the barn and the back of the ranchhouse, he reached a point where he could see the front door. Colt in hand, he scrambled up the bank. Then, putting his head down, he flew over the ground toward the steps.

The screams of the wounded man rang in the evening air. It was the Rio Kid's hope it might distract the men temporarily, for he had two hundred yards to cover to make the front porch. He ran like an Indian. He was within fifty yards of the house when a guard opened fire from a side window, up near the veranda. The Rio Kid felt the burn of the bullet on his left arm, and shot at the opening as he dashed in.

As he had figured, his shot from the rear, and the yelps of their companion had drawn most of the men to the rear of the house, which gave him precious moments in which to reach the front porch. Colt blasting that window, the Rio Kid dived past the turn and leaped to the door.

Two men were waiting for him, and he glimpsed one throwing up his gun just inside the opening. He fired, and the bullet missed the moving Rio Kid, while his own answering shot doubled the gunman up. Keeping low down, with his teeth gleaming as he fought, the Rio Kid jumped into the room. Pistols roared, echoing in the confined space, and then the second gunny crashed.

He knocked over the heavy-topped oak table, crouching behind it. He was just in time, for five more men came pushing up from the kitchen, warned by the shots and the howls of the two left at the windows up front. His bold play, almost insane in its recklessness, had been something they had not guessed he would dare try. It forced

152

them to come to him, and he had cover from which to fight.

Cool as a cucumber, the Rio Kid saw the huge Ole Stensen lumber through the connecting door, swearing in a great bellow of fury. Stensen had a gun in one paw. His evil eyes touched on his writhing, wounded followers, and then he saw the brassy-nerved Rio Kid close on him.

"Throw down, Stensen," ordered Pryor. "Yuh're my prisoner!"

"The Rio Kid!" shouted Stensen, chin dropping. He stared stupidly for an instant, flabbergasted at sight of his foe inside the house.

"Get him!" shrieked a black-bearded fellow behind Ole. "He's alone — get him!"

Stensen's Colt muzzle swung on the Rio Kid. But Pryor beat him to the shot, and Stensen's pistol went off before it was fully up, the slug burrowing into the floor. The big fellow took the Rio Kid's lead in the forehead, and his head snapped back. A moment later he folded up in a heap, blocking the door.

Roars of rage sounded from the throats of his men.

"C'mon — get in there — kill him!" shouted Black-beard.

They charged, and the Rio Kid, down

153

behind the table, heard the rapping of bullets in the wood. He fired from one side, then from the other. Two men took his lead, stopped, and then they turned tail and ran back through the connecting door.

"Boys — every man up front and get him!" he heard the lieutenant shout, taking command now that Ole Stensen was dead.

Heavy feet shook the house. Every man was concentrating on the Rio Kid now. Pryor whistled, shrill blasts that were ear-piercing.

As they began shooting at him again, however, he heard a Rebel yell, and explosions from outside. Bigfoot Wallace and Arthur Barron came charging from the barn and made for the kitchen door. They began shooting into the bunch at the center of the house, and these men split up like a flock of alarmed birds. Several reached the side windows, jumped out, and ran for their saddled horses.

Sounding his war-cry, the Rio Kid leaped to his feet and hurried them on their way. They went galloping off across the creek, led by the black-bearded man. Nine survivors there were, and five dead men had been left behind.

Bigfoot Wallace, grinning, rushed up to shake the Rio Kid's hand.

"I knowed we'd get outa that hole!" he crowed.

Barron's face was pale, drained of blood. He had a fresh bullet wound in his upper right arm, and he had not entirely recovered from the injuries he previously had received. Bigfoot had several minor hurts, and was covered with blood, powder smudge and chaff, but he was in high spirits.

"Where's Mireles?" demanded the Rio Kid, wiping the blood from his face. He had three tears in his hide from the terrific scrap.

"He's got one in the leg," replied Bigfoot, turning and heading for the kitchen. "Boy, I'm starved. I been eatin' dried corn and hay for the last twenty-four hours, Rio Kid."

"We tried to get out after dark last night," Barron explained. "They shot down two of the horses, though, and Celestino couldn't run. We had to go back in the barn. It was mighty hot while it lasted."

They trailed Wallace into the kitchen, on the way to the barn. Bigfoot was wolfing everything in sight, washing it down with big swigs from the whiskey bottle he had found on the table.

The Rio Kid's glance took in the kitchen. There were pegs on the wall, and he saw some eagle feather head-dresses, some

Indian headbands and clothing. On a shelf stood a big can filled with dark berry juice.

"Huh!" he growled. "Reckon there are yore Indians, Barron. Whites fixed up like redskins raided yuh that night."

"You're right," agreed Barron.

"We better get outa here," the Rio Kid said.

"Aw, what's the hurry," said Bigfoot. "I'm still hungry."

"There'll be more comin' to start battlin' again. So hustle."

Pryor passed through the back door. Mireles, leaning against the door post, sang out gayly to him.

"General! I knew you'd come eef posseeble! But I feared, too, you might be dead."

Pryor hurried to his Mexican comrade. Celestino had been hit in the right leg the night before and it would not hold his weight. But he could ride a horse, painful though it might be.

Shrill whistles, bars of the song the dun loved. "Said the Big Black Charger to the Little White Mare!" brought Saber galloping up. The Rio Kid, forcing Wallace to desert the fleshpots, got his friends mounted.

"Let's take what's left of Barron's hosses,

at least," said Bigfoot.

They drove the animals out, but before they could get started, the Rio Kid, watching the sky toward Hannigan's town, saw dust in the air. It was too far away to be from the hoofs of the fleeing cowboys of the Circle S.

"Never mind them broncs now," he growled. "Head for Valcito, boys, and pronto."

He started them off, up the hill. Riding to pick up his carbine, he could see the dust cloud rapidly approaching the Circle S. No doubt the men he had gunned out of the place would meet the reinforcements and tell them what had occurred. Which was all the more reason for haste.

Lagging behind his friends, the Rio Kid, in the last of the daylight, saw a large band of riders break up from the creek ford and gallop for the ranch.

Chapter XV
The Rio Kid's Play

Night fell, and the stars twinkled out. The Rio Kid rode on slowly, through the black woods. Now and then the slice of moon penetrated its silver light to the trail. He kept looking back, listening. Reaching the road across the mountain to Valcito, he went forward at a walk, waiting.

Mireles and Barron could not ride over-fast, injured as they were, and he figured that there might be pursuit by the enraged cowmen.

He was right. But it came even sooner than expected. He heard the beat of a couple of hundred hoofs, on the road behind him. They had taken a shortcut and were riding fast, evidently aware of the direction in which the quartet would head.

Up at a gap where the road turned, the Rio Kid stopped, and from the shadows watched the long, moonlit slope behind. Masses of riders appeared, spurring their horses on the blood-trail.

The Rio Kid waited until they were within two hundred yards, then opened fire with his carbine. Two riders in the van crashed, and hoarse commands were bellowed, the force splitting and riding off into cover at the sides of the road.

Having given them pause, he rode swiftly on, but waited for them at another bend. It was twenty minutes before a single rider gingerly rounded the curve, and ducked as the Rio Kid's lead shrieked past his ear.

They took to the rocks, trying to circle him, but he moved on.

After two hours of this, he found a wide trail off the main road, and with stinging bullets caused them to follow. They were blood-angry and believed he was the rear guard of the quartet. He doubled back, and came out on the road, making for the town of Bubbling Springs. His friends now had such a long start that they could not be overtaken before reaching Valcito, and so he allowed the dun to have his head, riding under the stars.

Stopping after a couple of miles, he rolled a cigarette and had a smoke. It was pleasing after his long and arduous exertion.

"I'd like to know where them reinforcements come from, and that setup's mighty interestin'," he told Saber.

His keen ears caught the sound of hoofs. He started to ride on, but soon saw only a single rider was approaching, so he drew into the brush and waited.

A man rode by, hunched over his horse. His face was darkly bearded, and the Rio Kid thought it was the same one he had met at Stensen's — the lieutenant he had mentally dubbed Black-beard.

When he was gone, the Rio Kid took the road again and followed. . . .

It was the dark hour before dawn. Jed Hannigan walked the floor, cursing in his impatience. Egghead's messenger, a renegade Ute, had left an hour ago, to return to Pete with Hannigan's further orders.

At last Hannigan heard hoofbeats, and a man rode up to the back door and dismounted. It was "Blacky" Durgan, Ole Stensen's right-hand man and chief lieutenant.

"It's about time Ole reported," snarled Hannigan, and shut the door on Blacky.

He lit a candle, shading it with a basket.

"Everybody's asleep in this tarnation town. Still I ain't anxious to show a light this time of night. . . . Well, did Jake Phillips and his men arrive? I hope sixty of yuh was able to take them three fools in the barn!"

Hannigan rubbed his right ear, remembering how close that slug had come to killing him the previous night, when he had gone out to the Circle S to help take Bigfoot Wallace and his two pards. The scab had formed but it still tingled, and he would carry a scar there.

"Yeah, Phillips come, but not in time, Chief," growled Blacky. "Ole, he's dead. The Rio Kid kilt him."

"The Rio Kid!"

The unhappy tale came out and left Hannigan cursing in his fury.

"Where's that gang now?" he asked finally, catching himself.

"Comin' in. I rode ahead to report to yuh. We lost 'em in the dark."

"I'll take care of the Rio Kid later, then, blast him! No time to fool with him now. I was lucky to pick up Phillips and his bunch. They was just startin' over into Arizona on a raidin' tour of the ranches there. He'll fight with us, but I have to pay on the nose for every man. You take charge, Blacky. I'll tell Phillips and his rustlers to fight as you order. Smear up as Indians and join Egghead Pete at the spring half a mile east of Skeleton Peak, savvy? Report to Egghead and he'll have command over all. Manuel

Perez is camped near there. Yuh're to attack his force and lead it onto the guns of the Navajos and Apaches. Wolfkiller and Victorio have nearly two thousand braves and are ready to hit. They'll overrun Manuel Perez, and sweep on to battle with Francisco, 'fore they join."

"All right, Jed. But if I ever get a crack at that Rio Kid devil —" Blacky cursed fluently.

"We'll take care of him later. Far as them hosses go, we'll cover up. Yuh can always say yuh bought 'em from Indians and yuh thought the hombres who came at yuh were rustlers."

In the distance, hoofbeats shook the ground. The rustler gang of Jake Phillips, and the survivors of Stensen's Circle S were returning after their fruitless chase of the Rio Kid.

And the Rio Kid himself, with an ear pressed to the crack of Jed Hannigan's rear door, decided it was time to fade into the shadows. He picked up the hidden dun and, leading him away from the settlement into the chaparral, mounted and silently stole off, to hit the road for Valcito.

When finally he arrived at Valcito, with the dun steaming in the cool of the small hours, he found that his three comrades had reached the Perez *hacienda* safely.

Lanterns shimmered in the dark, for armed sentries were out. Don Francisco had left a force of *vaqueros* guarding the homes and the loved ones in them. Passed through the lines when he identified himself, Pryor made for the *hacienda*. He took care of his horse first, then drank, and located Bigfoot Wallace who was dozing in the *patio*.

"Oof!" grunted Bigfoot, rubbing his eyes and yawning prodigiously. "I'm plumb wore out, Rio Kid. We got here all right but yore Mex pard has a mighty sore leg. I'm sorry I run 'em into all that fuss at the Circle S."

"I ain't," the Rio Kid said promptly. "It's workin' out fine, Bigfoot. Has Kit Carson got here yet?"

"Yep. Him and Frémont pulled in durin' the afternoon. They say Kit's sufferin' a lot from his hurt chest but he just would ride over. He fetched along a dozen Ute braves, pards of his from Taos. Yuh savvy he's takin' special care of the Utes over there. And by criminy, if Gen'ral Sherman, red beard and all, didn't stroll in with Kit! His cavalry escort's camped on t'other side of the square.

"Sherman was on an inspection tour, and heard of the Navajo uprisin' when he hit Fort Lyon, across the Colorado line. He give orders immediately for troops to foller, and he lit out to Kit Carson's. He come over here with Kit."

"I've got to wake Kit and talk with him," said the Rio Kid. "I hate to rouse him, when he's feelin' bad, but it has to be done. Where will I find him sleepin'?"

"Over in that wing, third room," Bigfoot told him.

The Rio Kid strolled over. His secret information was too urgent to wait and he knew that Carson would not thank him for failing to turn it in at once. Opening a panel door, he stepped into a long corridor and counted the doors until he came to the third. As he stopped, supple, dark figures leaped up, seizing his arms. A knife point was pressed against his back.

"What — what?" a hoarse-voice grunted in his ear, as the startled Rio Kid felt the prick of steel.

"Hey — what the devil!" he snarled.

His captors were big Indians, in buckskin and warpaint. They had been lying along the wall outside Carson's room.

He addressed them in Navajo, but they only grunted back.

"Ute — Ute," said the leader.

"Where's Father Kit? *Amigo* — friend."

"Friend? Go 'way. Father Kit he sleep."

Carson's voice came to them, speaking in the Ute tongue. The Ute chief replied.

"It's me, Kit," called Pryor. "I got to see yuh."

Carson gave an order and instantly the clutching, powerful hands released him, and the knife was snatched back.

"Come in," Carson sang out.

The Rio Kid pushed through the door. Kit Carson struck a sulphur match, which fumed and smoked. When its flame came up he touched it to a candle by his bedside. Sitting up in bed, Carson showed the ordeal he had undergone. His face was scabbed and sore from the scraping, and he held his shoulders hunched over. But he was the sort of man who could rise above pain.

"I hope my Utes didn't upset yuh," he said. "They're trusted men, every one, and my bodyguard. I didn't fetch 'em with me before because the Utes are more or less hereditary enemies of the Navajos, and I didn't want to antagonize Wolfkiller, not while there was any chance of peace."

"Sherman's here, I understand," said the Rio Kid.

Kit Carson nodded, sadly, pursing his lips.

"Yes. He's ordered out infantry and a battery of field guns, plus the cavalry. I've got to scout for the Army, of course, now it's come to a showdown. It's up to me to locate the Indians and lead the soldiers to 'em. I hate to do it because it's bound to mean death and destruction for the Navajos."

"I got new information, Kit," Pryor said slowly, watching his friend's drawn face. "Dunno whether it's too late or not, but there's a faint chance of checkin' the war, if only we could reach Wolfkiller and his chiefs 'fore the big scrap opens up. Remember that Gasca hombre we killed? I've found who he was workin' for, and I've found who's bossin' Egghead Pete and his renegades. There's some whites in it, too, and they've hit both sides, Navajos and settlers, and made all this trouble."

Carson's shrewd old gray-blue eyes narrowed.

"Go on." he growled.

"His name," the Rio Kid continued, "is Jed Hannigan. Yuh savvy who he is?"

Carson started violently. "Hannigan! Yuh mean the trader and newspaper editor below? Why should he do such things?"

The Rio Kid shrugged. "I ain't shore of his reason, Kit. He's cleanin' up plenty, of course, sellin' war supplies to Perez and his friends."

Kit shook his head. "That don't altogether make it. But then, there is a lot in such business. It's been done before, though not to such an extent as this."

Chapter XVI
The Apache Way

Pressed for further details by Kit Carson, the Rio Kid described the way he had found his three friends gone, had tracked them to the Circle S, and had rescued them. He told how later he had overheard Hannigan giving orders to Blacky Durgan.

"Yuh savvy this rustler Jake Phillips, Kit?" he asked.

"Yeah. He's a tough customer, who'll throw his guns into any pot where he stands a chance to make some money. Now lemme think this all over. We've got to stop it, somehow. How long yuh reckon we have?"

"A few hours leeway, in case we start pronto. It'll take Blacky a while to contact Egghead Pete, and Phillips' men got to load up and get in position."

"Let's see — Blacky's to have Phillips' gang smear up as Indians. Then they'll meet Egghead Pete at the spring half a mile east of Skeleton Peak — I know the exact spot.

Egghead takes command. They attack Manuel Perez and lead him onto the Navajo rifles."

"That's it."

The Rio Kid's military brain had carefully memorized the details of Hannigan's strategy and so reported it to Kit Carson.

"S'pose," he went on, as Carson turned it over in his keen brain, "we was to beat Blacky's fighters to that spring and capture Egghead Pete? We got to show Wolfkiller this time. He was wounded by whites, Stensen's men, when he rode to the peak that day as he promised. Yuh reckon Wolfkiller'll be out with his braves?"

"It depends on how bad he's hurt." Kit Carson grunted with pain as he left his bed. "We'll chance it, Rio Kid. It may mean my death but I'll stop the war if I can. If I could contact Wolfkiller in the right way and show him, make him believe what yuh've told me — and Perez, too — that would be the way."

He began dressing. His chest hurt every time he moved, but he would let nothing check him. As a matter of fact, Kit Carson never entirely recovered from the effects of that terrible fall. When, some time later, he knew he was dying, when he was on a visit to Fort Lyon, Colorado Territory, he attributed it to those chest injuries he had

169

received.

"I'll start right away," Carson declared now, lacing his leather moccasin boots.

"I'm goin' with yuh," insisted the Rio Kid.

Carson shook his head. "It's practically shore death, if we're caught. And I mean to enter Wolfkiller's camp."

"Let me go!"

"I'm not takin' any fighters, at least not whites. My Utes will help me. They're all I'll need. And at the showdown I'll drop them."

"Let me go along!" the Rio Kid still pleaded, and Kit Carson finally gave in. "Yuh asked for it," he said. "Yuh're the only man I'd allow with me, Rio Kid. Get ready."

The Ute warriors were armed. Kit Carson saw to it that they had plenty of ammunition for their rifles. They wore supple boot-moccasins, deerskin leggings, and bands about their dark locks. They followed Carson like so many ferocious animals, ready to do his bidding.

Gray was touching the sky behind the *hacienda* when all was ready.

"Frémont would like to come," remarked Carson. "He loves new country. Any place he hasn't been, he'll snoop through. He's never still, always on the prowl. Got the habit when he was young and can't get over it. Those were great days, Rio Kid, when Frémont and I broke through a thousand miles of virgin wilderness, Utah and California, and the immense territories."

He shook his head, sadly, thoughtfully reminiscent for a moment.

"I was strong then and full of beans," he said. "I could go for a week, fightin' on a bellyful of grass and a swaller of alkali water. I remember the first time we seen Great Salt Lake, and the fights with rovin' Injuns who'd never laid eyes on white men before. Frémont never faltered. He was a great leader, my boy. We did big things, they say.

"But time passes us by. Do yuh realize that when I was born Thomas Jefferson was President, and young Dan'l Boone was just startin' into Kentucky? The United States was a helpless little bunch of pore colonies east of the Alleghanies. Now it runs from sea to sea." He paused, and added, "A few years, and Frémont and me are old, good for nothin'."

"Yuh're still worth a million, Kit," declared the Rio Kid. "I'd scout with yuh 'fore anybody I ever met."

Kit Carson smiled. "Thanks, Rio Kid."

He coughed. His injured chest bothered him. A big Ute brave stepped up, and Carson leaned on him as he moved through the wide gate to the street.

"Have to speak to Gen'ral Sherman 'fore we start," he said.

A company of crack U. S. Cavalry was camped at the upper end of the plaza. Sherman, an old campaigner who loved the soldier's life, bivouacked with his men.

Carson and the Rio Kid went to the little tent where a guidon, stuck in the ground, waved three stars on it. Sentries challenged them, and a lieutenant, a fresh-faced young man, came out.

"I hate to disturb the general —" he began.

A sharp voice issued from Sherman's tent. "Who is it, Lieutenant?"

"Kit Carson, sir. He says he has an important message."

Sherman roused up, and came out of the tiny shelter, grunting as he smoothed his red beard and hair in the damp of the early morning.

Tall and spare, he was a fierce-eyed man with gaunt cheeks. He was past middle age but still wiry and competent to lead troops in the field.

"War is all they call it," he remarked, with rough joviality. "Especially when you have to get up at such an hour! What is it, Kit, my old friend?"

Sherman had often called upon Kit Carson and trusted him implicitly. As a scout, guide and Indian fighter, there had never been another to compare with Father Kit. Carson led him aside, speaking in a low tone.

Sherman frowned, shook his head.

"I can't let you do this, Kit. It would be practically certain death for you and anyone who goes along. My information has it that Victorio has joined the Navajos and that they have over two thousand warriors."

"The Rio Kid will be the only white man with me," argued Carson. "I've got to try, General. Mebbe I can save the people."

Sherman turned, nodding to Pryor, who came to attention and saluted. He knew Sherman, had seen him in the Army camps during the Civil War when Captain Robert Pryor had scouted for Custer.

"Very well, then, Kit," agreed Sherman, with a shake of his red-maned head. "My forces won't be up for five days, and I've got to wait here until then anyway. If I haven't heard from you by that time I'll conclude you've failed, and strike. I hate to lose you, because I need you to lead us."

"I'll give you the names of two men at Taos who can do it as well," promised Kit Carson. "But we must start, and now,

General, 'fore the mornin' mists are dispelled. I don't doubt but that the enemy has spies on the hilltops, watchin' this place."

As they were mounting, however, they were further delayed by the hurried arrival of Frémont, who had awakened to find Kit Carson leaving.

"I'd like to go along, Kit," Frémont insisted.

Carson shook his head. "No, John. I wish I could take yuh, but it's impossible."

A large flock of sheep, driven by some of Don Francisco's herders, came across the plaza in the drifting gray mists. The Rio Kid stared at the animals. They had been fetched in from the nearby hills and dales to save them from marauders.

"Funny stains on their wool," he remarked, and Fremont, frowning, turned to look at the reddish blotches on the bleating creatures.

Frémont's eyes widened. "Yes — interesting."

He stepped to one of the shepherds and began to talk with him in easy lingo, asking exactly where the sheep had been grazing.

Without waiting to hear what was said, however, Kit Carson, the Rio Kid, and eight lithe Ute braves rode in the mists out of

Valcito by a side trail. There they took to the chaparral and headed for Skeleton Peak and the spring near the commanding spire.

It was night. The Utes moved through the black brush like so many silent snakes. There were only seven of the Indians now, and with Kit Carson and the Rio Kid there were nine men in the party. The tenth had been left half a mile back with the muzzled mustangs, well-hidden.

The Rio Kid and the chief of the Utes, O-Ke-Bah, had been detailed to seize Egghead Pete, no matter what. The rest were to attack and overwhelm, if possible, the forces with the renegade. They could not guess how many men Egghead might have with him. He usually traveled with a dozen of his own stamp but he could have augmented his band in the days since they had fought him across the wilderness.

The Rio Kid crawled just behind O-Ke-Bah, a powerful Ute who had served Kit Carson since the scout had adopted him when the Indian's parents had been killed in a flood on the Snake River. Carson, lip bitten between his teeth to stifle the pain he felt in his chest, came at the rear, helped by his Indian friends. He had insisted on being with the attacking party, refusing to remain with the horses.

Armed to the teeth, they approached foot by foot, the gleaming spring in the wooded hollow below, stopping to listen with bated breath. Half a mile to the west, Skeleton Peak thrust its shadowed summit toward the night sky.

As carefully as possible, they had figured out the timing. Blacky and the rustler, Phillips, would need time to rest their men, and get them fixed up as Indians so they could pass as such at a distance in the battle they planned, to hand out plenty of ammunition and other necessary gear, and then ride to the spring. From what the Rio Kid had learned, Egghead Pete was expecting Hannigan to send him these reinforcements, so he would undoubtedly visit the spring to receive them.

O-Ke-Bah and the Rio Kid were some yards in advance of the line. Inching painfully forward, keeping down flat so they would not bulk against the moon, sky and stars, avoiding dry sticks and brush that might rustle, they approached the big spring.

Stopping to listen again, they could hear not the slightest sound. Resuming progress, O-Ke-Bah and Pryor reached the damp earth on the outskirts of the tiny clearing with the spring, and, after careful reconnoitering, began to circle it.

It was altogether deserted and the trained fingers, nose and eyes of the Ute did not find the smallest clue to tell that men had been there within the past two days.

The Rio Kid swung, and crawled back to report this disappointing news to Kit Carson.

"We'll wait," whispered Father Kit. "They will come, if yuh heard aright, Rio Kid. We can rest, hide ourselves and be ready. We figgered that Blacky Durgan and Jake Phillips couldn't make it here before noon tomorrow. Egghead would savvy that, too, and he wouldn't pull in here till . . . Ssh!"

They froze, listening. The night wind, from the direction of Skeleton Peak and the wild mountains, brought them a faint sound.

Eyes intent on the crest, blackly wooded to the ridge top, where jagged rocks were painted against the lighter sky, the Rio Kid saw the figure of a rider etched for an instant. Then another, and more and more, crossing over and dropping out of sight in the shadowed, inky basin.

Without speaking, Kit Carson telegraphed his order by a touch, relayed to the rest. The nine men melted into the brush, flattening themselves against the cold earth.

"Hoo! Hoo-hoo! Hoo! Hoo-hoo!"

They could hear the low, guttural grunting of the Indians riding in on them, so sure of their ground they suspected not the slightest danger. And it was an Apache way, to sing-song that way to the rhythm of a mustang's motion!

CHAPTER XVII
THE SCALES OF DEATH

Only a hundred yards out from the gleaming pool, the horsemen dismounted. Two shadowy figures flitted through a narrow deer trail, up to the brink, and then called softly back.

The mustangs were led up, to be watered, while the riders lay flat to drink.

In vain the Rio Kid sought to identify Egghead Pete among the fifteen silent, ebony figures gathered at the spring. It was too dark and they all looked alike at even a couple of yards distance, in the shadowed bush.

He heard low grunts, Indian talk, no doubt orders.

Suddenly, after faint rustlings, a match was struck. It flared up like a signal glow from a dark pit, lighting the band of painted, hard-eyed renegades, many of them breeds of two or three tribes, some of Mexican or American strain mixed with the red blood of savage ancestors.

The man who had struck the sulphur match, which smoked and sputtered, held it to the cigarette he had rolled. The glow lighted up the evil, horrible face of Egghead Pete. The renegade had learned the white man's way of smoking, and had the habit.

This little diversion from usual Indian caution was of immense help to the Rio Kid and his friends; it nailed Egghead Pete for O-Ke-Bah and Pryor, and placed the rest of them right where they squatted. Having drunk, they pulled out rations from their pouches and began to eat.

The Rio Kid touched O-Ke-Bah's bronzed, muscular arm. It was the signal, and an instant later Pryor launched himself across the space separating him from Egghead Pete, with O-Ke-Bah's powerful figure close at his side.

About a dozen feet, three or four leaps, were between the Rio Kid and his special prey.

The stunning, startling attack from the brush, and the realization that their enemies were right in their midst as they believed themselves safe at the watering place, held Egghead Pete's followers spellbound for one awful instant. The Rio Kid, lunging forward with all the weight of his strong body, hit

Pete in the chest, knocking him back into the water, then landing on him.

The cigarette flew from the renegade's lips, hissing out instantly in the spring. Egghead went under, with the Rio Kid on top of him, while O-Ke-Bah lashed in beside him, reaching for the renegade's struggling, fighting arms.

"Throw up yore hands!" Kit Carson shouted, as water made splashing sounds in the night.

But the renegades were already snatching up guns. Pistols and carbines blared, and bullets bit into the chaparral.

The Rio Kid, with one hand on Egghead Pete's scrawny, pulsing throat, held on like a bulldog, refusing to let go. He was trying to get his other hand to the cartilage and throttle Egghead entirely, but Pete was slashing at him wildly with his fingernails, gouging at his eyes and cheeks. He kept kneeing the Rio Kid, and rolling.

On the bank behind him, the shooting rose to a horrid crescendo. Men fired point-blank at their foes. Colts and short-barreled rifles were used, but the attackers had the advantage, knowing where their foes were for the opening shots.

Kit Carson and his Utes fought savagely, ruthlessly, now that the die was cast. Their

181

guns had ripped into the bunched renegades of Egghead Pete, and four of the latter went down in the first volley.

Carson rose up, shooting as he charged. His Utes slashed in, at close quarters, pistols and knives working fast.

The Rio Kid heard lead singing right over his head. Egghead Pete, sputtering, sought to get his nose above water for another breath of precious air. O-Ke-Bah, wallowing in the stirred mud of the spring, seized hold of Pete's right arm and bent it back, while the Rio Kid, riding on Egghead and keeping him down, slid along.

"No kill, O-Ke-Bah!" gasped the Rio Kid, as he saw a knife gleam in the Ute's sinewy hand.

"No kill!" the Ute growled.

The others were not under that compulsion. At rapid-fire, they had downed half of Egghead Pete's force, while the rest tried to scatter, to escape, appalled by the terrible in-fighting and savagery of their foes.

But the Utes were ready. Only two of Carson's men had felt lead, and the others sprang after the renegades, bringing them down before they could reach their ponies.

Save for the whining of two wounded breeds, silence suddenly dropped over the black basin. Silence save for the fainter and fainter splashings made by Egghead Pete and the Rio Kid as they fought in the cold water.

"Rio Kid — need help?"

That was Kit Carson, squatting on the bank, the breath rasping painfully in and out of his lungs.

"No — no —"

Egghead Pete went limp in his clutch. The Rio Kid lifted the dripping renegade quickly up, and threw him, head down over one shoulder with O-Ke-Bah's assistance. Water poured out of Pete's open mouth.

Wading in, the Rio Kid dumped his prisoner at Kit Carson's feet.

"Shake — the water — out," he gasped.

He flung himself down, to get back his breath. The cold of the night pierced to his wet skin.

Carson's Utes had tied and gagged their captives, and were dragging them into a line close at hand, working rapidly. Five of Egghead Pete's men were dead; six wounded.

"Fix it," ordered Father Kit in the Ute tongue, "so that the white men who come later will not notice that anything has happened here."

His men obediently set about erasing signs. The dead were carried and hidden in dense thickets, mud was smoothed over, and the wounded and prisoners taken to their horses, and tied on the mustangs.

Half a dozen of the Utes took charge of them, while the Rio Kid, O-Ke-Bah and Kit Carson, with Egghead Pete as their prisoner, hurried back to where they had left their horses. O-Ke-Bah carried Egghead. They had rolled as much water out of him as they could, and he was still alive, was muttering, coming back to his senses.

The Rio Kid helped the injured Carson up the slope. He needed help, for only his spirit drove Kit Carson on. The hurt in his chest was worse, from the terrific exertion of the battle, but he would not quit. Human lives must be saved, and Kit Carson would keep on to the end.

Scratches and bruises were the only injuries that Pryor had received. Carson had a knife gash in his hand, which bled annoyingly, but it was a superficial wound. O-Ke-Bah had come off with only a wetting.

As for Egghead Pete, their prize for which they had taken such reckless chances, with the scales of death threatening to balance against them, he was only knocked out. The Rio Kid had pulled him from the water before he drowned.

As Egghead came fully back to consciousness and began fighting at O-Ke-Bah, they paused to gag him, and to fasten his hands and ankles.

Reaching their horses, the quartet mounted. Kit Carson rode his powerful gray, the Rio Kid was riding Saber, and O-Ke-Bah's mount was a beautiful dark-hided chestnut. Egghead Pete was slung over the blanketed back of a Ute mustang and tied securely in position.

The Ute who had kept watch over the horses was told to wait for his comrades, who would soon be along with the injured and captives. Then Kit Carson and the Rio Kid, with O-Ke-Bah leading the black mustang to which the helpless, frightened Egghead Pete was tied, started into the Navajo hills.

Perilous as had been the job at the spring, they were on their way to attempt another feat far more dangerous — one that seemed practically impossible. They would need every bit of their skill, their training, and luck besides to balance the scales of death in their favor this time.

The dawn came slowly up, and they were able to see, from the ridge along which they were riding, some of the country to the west and ahead. It was majestic Navajo country of buttes, and mountains and small waterholes. Vast rock formations of vari-colored hues gleamed in the rising sunlight.

They chewed jerky as they rode, headed for the Chest of the Serpents. Egghead Pete, his misshapen head bobbing with the motion against the barrel ribs of the mustang he was tied to, watched the grim-faced Rio Kid and Kit Carson, and the breed's slanted black eyes glowed with fear.

He had lost his nerve, after his near-drowning at the hands of Bob Pryor and O-Ke-Bah, and expected at any moment to be put to death. Their silence, and their air of determination, increased his nervousness. He did not know what was to happen.

Late in the afternoon, riding doggedly on, guided by Kit Carson's marvelous instinct for geography and his knowledge of the country, O-Ke-Bah pointed to a low ravine distantly visible in the west, on their right as they moved.

"Apaches — Navajos — like leaves in the forest," he reported to Carson.

"Move to the other side of the ridge," commanded Kit Carson. "We mustn't be seen by them."

Out of sight, they stopped.

"I must know if Wolfkiller, Chief of the People, the Navajos, is with them down there," Carson said. "He was wounded, mebbe hurt so bad he can't ride."

"Let me go," the Rio Kid said at once.

"Very well, Rio Kid. But — I need yuh. Have a care. As for me, I must rest, so we'll wait here till yuh come back."

Two hours later, the Rio Kid lay on the edge of a great cliff, its lip covered with scrub brush, dropping five hundred feet to the rocky ravine bottom below.

He saw more Indians than he had ever seen in his life before at one time. There were Apaches, fierce-eyed, head-banded fellows, and Navajos, with their copper bracelets and turquoise studs. There were Utes and Pai-Utes, who were ready to fight with their former enemies against the whites.

"Must be a couple thousand of 'em!" marveled the Rio Kid.

They were camped, now, and feeding. Great bands of hairy mustangs showed close at hand. Groups of heavily armed warriors lounged about, as they ate and drank. His trained military eye took in their arms and gear, their evident hostile intent.

Creeping back, he reached the dun and rode the miles to Kit Carson's side, reporting.

"Wolfkiller ain't with 'em."

The two-hour respite had made it possible for Carson to keep going.

"Then he must be at the Chest of the Serpents," muttered Carson. "So much the better for us."

Wearily, painfully, Carson mounted. They slung Egghead Pete over his mustang, and shoved on.

CHAPTER XVIII
BIG GAMBLE

Dark had fallen when Kit Carson called a halt.

"O-Ke-Bah," he said softly, to his faithful Ute follower, in the Indian's own language, "we must part here. Wait for me until this time tomorrow. If we don't come, make your way back to Sorrel-beard, General Sherman, and tell him we are dead and he must attack as he wills, that there is no help for it."

The Chest of the Serpents lay about half a mile to the west. It was there that Kit Carson meant to make his way in the darkness.

"Yuh're shore yuh can carry Egghead Pete?" Carson asked the Rio Kid. "It's rough goin'."

The Rio Kid nodded. He was ready to follow Kit Carson to the inferno and back.

Their prisoner was in a dither of fear. His limbs ached from the tight rawhides that bound them and the gag made his ugly eyes

189

bulge out. The Rio Kid slung him over his shoulder, and Kit Carson took the lead.

They were gambling everything on this play. If they failed, they would never escape themselves, and the terrible war would flare into consuming flame.

Approaching with animal stealth, they reached the brink of the wild, wooded canyon where the Navajos were hiding. Kit Carson, who knew the country like a book, dared not approach the main entrance. Instead, he had picked a steep rock slide some distance above the People's camp.

The Rio Kid had his hands full, with Egghead Pete over his shoulder. He tried, with his moccasined feet, to keep from sliding as the old scout showed the way down into the Chest of the Serpents.

A horrid, low hum, a rattler disturbed in his night hunt, came from nearby, but they quickly passed. The Rio Kid nearly lost his balance, but caught himself by his left hand against a jutting rock.

Then Kit Carson was down on the floor of the deep canyon. The low purl of water on stones helped drown the slight noises they made. Both men wore moccasins, supple coverings made from the softened hide of deer, and buckskin pants. They had tied their hair with bandannas, for their hats and shoes and noisy gear had been left with O-Ke-Bah and the horses.

The Rio Kid could feel Egghead Pete trembling like a leaf.

Slowly, with the only light coming from the stars and a bit of moon, Kit Carson felt his way down the Chest of the Serpents toward the camp of the People, the Navajos.

Bob Pryor, bent under Egghead's weight, heard the soft hiss of his companion, Kit Carson:

"Stay here till I come back."

He was glad of a pause. He laid his prisoner on the ground and squatted there, his shoulders aching from the unaccustomed drag on them.

It was half an hour before Kit Carson returned, and touched his arm.

"Wolfkiller is in his hogan. There are sentinels out but they're down toward the gate. The camp's asleep."

Fires had burned down to embers, with only a red coal glowing here and there. Keeping close to Carson's heels, the Rio Kid brought Egghead Pete as near as could be done behind a screen of scrub brush and rocks.

"We'll have to make a run for it from here," Carson breathed in his ear. "If I can

reach Wolfkiller before the others catch us
—"

He paused for only a moment more, listening intently.

"Now!" he ordered, and ran lightly across the fifty yards of open ground toward the dark shape of Wolfkiller's hogan.

The Rio Kid started with him, with Egghead Pete bouncing on his shoulder. Suddenly a Navajo guard, beyond the hogan, saw the silent, dark figures headed for the leader's shelter. He uttered a warning yell and a shot whistled within inches of the moving scouts.

But Carson was already at the hide-hung entry.

"Wolfkiller — wake up!" he shouted in Navajo. "It is Father Kit!"

There was an answer, in the Navajo tongue, from the hogan. The chief had roused at the shot and heard Carson's frantic call.

"Don't shoot, Wolfkiller!" Kit warned. "We are unarmed and we bring you the answer to a riddle."

"Enter," Wolfkiller replied.

Braves were dashing up, to reach for the intruders, but at Wolfkiller's command, they fell back.

The Rio Kid pushed Egghead Pete inside

the hogan. The warm odor of hides and skins, and of the savages, permeated the confined space.

"Wolfkiller," Kit Carson said rapidly, close to the leader, "I have brought you a present. It is peace."

"No peace!" grunted Wolfkiller. "It is war. The white men have declared it."

"You must listen to me! Let me strike a light."

Wolfkiller gave his permission and Carson quickly lighted a candle stub he had brought in his pocket, ready for this, and set it on a flat stone.

The Rio Kid crouched down, over Egghead Pete, and the Navajo leader's black eyes flickered as he saw the renegade, trussed and a prisoner.

"Why do you do that?" he asked Carson. "The Man-Whose-Mother-Dropped-Him is an ally of the Navajos."

"No! He is your enemy and my enemy. He is the key to the riddle."

"How?" asked the chief.

"Listen and he will tell you himself."

In English, Kit Carson said to the Rio Kid: "Ungag him and hold this knife at his back."

He returned again to the Indian tongue, so that Wolfkiller and Egghead Pete might comprehend:

"If he lies, plunge the knife into his heart. We know everything. We know that Hannigan, the white trader at Bubbling Springs, is a thief, a liar and a killer. It was he who ordered this renegade to fire on the men of Valcito, and blame the killings on the Navajos. It was he who ordered the white rancher Stensen and his men to fire on the Navajos and lead the trail to Valcito."

Wolfkiller, who had been shot through the leg at Skeleton Peak by Stensen's gunmen, lay on a magnificent grizzly bear hide, his injured limb stretched straight out. He rested his head on one hand, while he listened. At his command, his guards remained outside the hogan.

"You see how much I know," Carson growled to Egghead Pete. "There is no use in your lying now. If you do, the Rio Kid will kill you instantly. You deserve it. You've murdered a dozen innocent people."

To the leader, Kit Carson said: "This man and his renegades ambushed me on my way to Valcito, after seeing you, my son. Because of him I am greatly hurt. My chest is crushed and it hurts me to breathe and to ride. See my face? When I went down, his bullet striking my horse, I was badly injured. Senor Perez never got your message to come to Skeleton Peak, and did not know you would be there. But this man told Hannigan so he could send his tools to kill you."

The Rio Kid had cut the gag from Egghead Pete's lips. Pete worked his face, clicking his lips to loosen the stiffened muscles.

"Talk, blast yuh," muttered the Rio Kid, the knife point pressed against Egghead's back, close under the heart.

"If you lie, you die," Kit Carson declared. "If you speak the truth, I will stand between you and the white man's law and do all that can be done for you, so that you shall have a fair trial."

Egghead Pete's nerve had cracked long before. He licked his lips, his sullen eyes darting from face to face. Wolfkiller was staring at him intently. And Egghead knew that the leader believed Father Kit. Carson had never lied to the Indians and had always tried to help them out of their numerous troubles.

"What Father Kit says is the truth," Egghead Pete said, in a low voice. "The white trader, Hannigan, told me to foment a war between the Navajos and the people of Valcito. Stensen, the rancher, too, was paid by Hannigan, and so were all our men. When Father Kit tried to settle the war, I did not want it settled, nor did Hannigan."

"Why did he want a war?" asked Carson.

Egghead Pete shrugged. "You can kill me if you want, but I don't know why the white trader wanted the fighting. I wanted it because I hate most white men and because I like war. I did what he told me."

Details came out as Egghead Pete was pressed. Already he had surrendered in his mind, and had given himself up for dead when Kit Carson and the Rio Kid had captured him. He told how his renegades and Stensen's gang had kept the fighting going by cunning, murderous tricks.

"I believe," Wolfkiller grunted at last. "Enough. I must call back my warriors. It will be hard, for the Apaches are ready for war and so are my braves."

"If they want a fight," the Rio Kid suggested, "why not send 'em to meet this Jake Phillips and Blacky's gang at the spring, Kit?"

"*Bueno,*" agreed Kit. "And the Perez faction must be warned. I am plumb wore out, Rio Kid. I must rest, here with my son, Wolfkiller. Find our friend O-Ke-Bah and have him tell Don Francisco the war is settled."

On one of Wolfkiller's mustangs, the Rio Kid left the Chest of the Serpents, while the leader dispatched trusted messengers with word to his war chiefs, giving his orders.

Picking up O-Ke-Bah in the night, the Rio Kid switched to Saber. Taking the lead, he rode on the back-trail.

CHAPTER XIX
SHOW-DOWN

For over twenty-four hours Blacky Durgan and Jake Phillips had been waiting, and still no sign of Egghead Pete. With Phillips, a huge, bloated-faced outlaw whose love of the whiskey bottle kept him in a semi-drunken state most of the time, Durgan paced restlessly on the path beaten near the spring.

"I dunno what to do, Jake!" Durgan complained for the hundredth time. "Egghaid's s'posed to take over from here. We was to attack Perez at Skeleton Peak but he won't lay there forever."

"Mebbe Pete got his," growled Jake. "A renegade like him don't live any too long."

Phillips' face was smeared with berry dye, and he had on buckskin and a Navajo headband, in simulation of a savage. His men, lounging about the spring, were also made up as Indians, their faces stained.

Three-score whites, killers and Frontier

desperadoes, owing allegiance only to the outlaw chieftain who paid them their blood money and led them on murderous adventures, were in the brush-choked basin. Their mustangs were close at hand.

They carried carbines and two revolvers apiece, with belts of ammunition for these weapons, and were ready for any sort of dirty job. Hannigan had considered himself fortunate to have enlisted such a powerful bunch of gunnies.

"Be blowed if I'll wait any longer," Blacky decided. "We better sashay over there and lay into Perez now."

"All right with me," agreed the bandit chieftain. "We're honin' for a scrap, Blacky. We'll rip 'em to pieces in no time."

He took a long swig of liquor from his flask, and swung to his hard-eyed followers.

"Get set, boys. We're goin' over to Skeleton Peak and wipe out Perez and his Mexes. Shoot to kill and keep yoreselves under cover. Yuh're Navajos, and Apaches, and don't forget it. Whoop it up some while yuh're shootin'."

Blacky had remained up the slope a bit, and Jake Phillips heard him exclaim in relief.

"Hey, Jake — here come some of Egghead's Injuns!"

The rustler leader turned to look. He saw

bronzed, naked savages break over the ridge and swarm along the trail, and as they sighted the killers, a shrill whoop rang over the basin.

"I don't see Egghaid Pete with 'em," declared Jake Phillips. "They look more like hostiles on the prowl to me."

Bullets began shrieking over them in the warm air. One of Jake's men swore shrilly and rolled over, kicking his legs.

"Stop that, yuh dang fools!" roared Blacky Durgan, and then his bearded chin dropped and his eyes opened as round as saucers. "The — the Rio Kid! He's leadin' them redskins!"

He turned and ran for his life. He had just seen the lithe figure of Bob Pryor, his chestnut-haired head bound with a Navajo head-band, running with gun in hand toward him, among the swift Indians bent on revenge.

"The whole place is swarmin' with 'em!" groaned Jake Phillips, aghast. "Somethin's gone sour, Blacky. We got to fight for our necks now."

From all along the ridges, and in the upper brush, armed Indians were leaping up, grim-eyed Navajos and some of their Apache allies.

"Fight, boys, fight!" quavered Jake Phillips, shuddering. "Cut yore way out, it's a trap."

His men, up on their feet, threw their carbines to shoulder and let go at the rushing savages, who were urged on by Bob Pryor, the Rio Kid. The Kid's Colts roared, reaching out steel fingers of death for the leaders of the renegades.

Jake Phillips was knocked around by a slug from the Rio Kid's gun. He cursed in panic, with blood streaming from a punctured shoulder. His pistol banged, and went off wild in the air.

More and more Indians were coming in with the Rio Kid and the chiefs. They leaped from rock to rock, and hundreds on hundreds drove at the gang, with horrible whooshings.

The clash was audible as the streaking bands of redskins charged into the bunched killers of Jake Phillips, the rustler leader. Guns roared at point-blank range and knives flashed in the sun as they went at it hand-to-hand.

The Rio Kid swerved, teeth gleaming in the joy of the battle. He cut toward Jake Phillips, who was exhorting his followers to fight. Phillips' left arm hung helpless at his side, for he had been plugged by the Rio Kid, but he was firing his Colt with his right. Seeing Pryor coming at him, the ugly rustler bellowed in bull-like fury and swung his pistol muzzle on Pryor.

"Drop it, Phillips!" shouted Pryor. "Tell yore men to throw in their guns and I —"

"Cuss yore hide, Rio Kid!" shrieked the maddened outlaw.

His eyes blazed red and he lifted his thumb off the hammer-spur, but the Rio Kid lashed in, feet leaving the ground. The bullet sailed over his head that was tied up like an Indian's with his bandanna.

A breath later, the Rio Kid's Colt snapped and Jake Phillips' murderous career was punctuated with finality by the bullet from Pryor's weapon. He took it between his red-rimmed eyes, and his mouth opened as he gasped like a dying fish. His big body shuddered, his knees caved in, and he folded up on the earth.

The Rio Kid, checking him, found him quivering in death. He sprang over the outlaw, hunting Blacky.

Lithe Apaches paused to snatch Jake Phillips' scalp. The Rio Kid tore on. He found himself in the midst of a hand-to-hand struggle between twenty of his Indian friends and a bunch of Phillips' surviving bandits. Guns belched almost against flesh and long knives slashed red with blood.

Shrieks and oaths joined in the rattle of the terrible battle.

The Rio Kid, with several nicks in his flesh, drove through one flank, hunting for Blacky Durgan.

"Hannigan ain't here, that's a cinch," blazed through his mind. "He keeps away from the fightin' if he can."

He brushed the sweat and blood from his eyes, looking about in the confusion for Durgan.

"There he goes!"

Blacky, using his long legs, had not paused to fight the attackers, but had fled around the north end of the spring and was making a run for the horses. Leaping into saddle, he was off. He was digging his spurs in deep, and beating his mustang with his gun barrel, low over the animal in a frantic break to escape the deathtrap set for him by the Rio Kid.

He shot down an Apache who jumped up in his path. The Rio Kid dashed after him, holding his fire until he could make a sure hit.

Behind him, as he seized a big black from the bunch of mustangs, who were dancing and snorting in terror at the heavy gunfire, the Rio Kid heard the battle raging on. The outlaws would not surrender, but fought desperately, aware of what awaited them if they quit.

A great welter of savage bodies swarmed in the confined basin, pressing in on the gunmen, cutting off escape.

The Rio Kid drove up the winding, constricted path on Durgan's trail. Blacky glanced back. He was low on the horse hugging the animal and clinging to the mane with one hand, spurs driving so deep that blood spurted from the running beast's flanks.

He saw the Rio Kid coming and his eyes widened in terror. He aimed back, seeking to knock Pryor from his horse, but the jolting pace and the distance made sure aim impossible. The slug flew wide, and the Rio Kid picked up several yards as Durgan's mustang slowed during the shot.

"Get out of here!" shrieked Blacky Durgan, almost insane with his fear.

He had seen this implacable gunfighter, the Rio Kid, in action all too often, and did not fancy such a duel as was going on.

The Rio Kid never took his eyes off Durgan, as he rode with a master's touch up the slope on Blacky's trail.

The second one Durgan let go at him was closer, and as Durgan took his attention off the terrified animal under him to fire, the beast's hoof slipped on the lip of the rocky hill, and he nearly went down.

Blacky clutched at the saddle-horn and mane with both hands, to keep from being pitched off. Precious seconds lost by him were to the Rio Kid's good, and Pryor gained yards.

He threw up his Colt, as Blacky, regaining mastery over his mount, swung again to shoot.

Lifting his thumb from the hammer spur, the Rio Kid drove a slug through Blacky from under the right arm, raised to fire, to Durgan's left side. Blacky slewed around, his head and arm dropping. The mustang swerved, then Durgan's body fell off, dragging by a stirrup.

Checking him, finding his heart punctured and that the lieutenant of Hannigan was dead, the Rio Kid turned to stare down into the basin of death.

Fighting had all but ceased. The killers had met their match, had tasted their own bitter medicine. They had perished fighting, or had thrown in their guns, bleating for mercy.

"Now where in tarnation is Hannigan?" muttered the Rio Kid. "He's next."

Chapter XX
Mountain Mystery

General William Tecumseh Sherman looked at Kit Carson and smiled.

"You've won a great victory, Carson," he complimented. "You and the Rio Kid. I reckon it's the best kind, too, for you did it without a war and saved hundreds of innocent lives and the homes of many of New Mexico's settlers."

Once again Kit Carson, by a daring stroke and through the exercise of his great personality, a man beloved by savages he had befriended, had turned the trick. He had averted a bloody Indian war.

Wolfkiller and Francisco Perez had been brought together, and the difficulties causing the hostilities had been ironed out in the conference between the whites and the Navajo leaders. The People, the Navajos, who wandered over their ancient tribal lands, tending their flocks of sheep and herds of cattle and goats, had returned to their hogans in peace. Victorio and his Apaches had ridden back to the arid reaches of Arizona, there to continue their implacable fight against civilization.

Sherman had countermanded his orders for troops to be sent in. There was no need for a long, difficult campaign against the Navajos.

They were sitting in the great salon of Don Francisco's home that evening, toasting Kit Carson. General Sherman meant to ride at dawn, back to Colorado with his bodyguard. The red-headed chief of the Southwest Army divisions turned his burning eyes on the Rio Kid.

"I have a scouting job for you, Rio Kid. What do you mean to do in the next three months? Will you ride to Fort Lyon with me?"

"I'd sure like to, Gen'ral. But there is a little job yet to be done in these parts. Mebbe later —"

"All right. Whenever you can."

The Rio Kid had a newspaper bunched in his hand, given him by an inhabitant of Valcito who had just come in from Bubbling Springs, Jed Hannigan's town. On the front of the crude little four-sheet paper the Rio Kid's name was prominent. The smudged headline blared:

LOCAL RANCHER SLAIN BY
TEXAS GUNMAN!

And Hannigan had let himself go in the body of the story which read:

Ole Stensen, owner of the Circle S of this valley, was brutally slain by the Rio Kid, a Texas gunslick who has been infesting these parts the past two weeks or so. Caught in the act of stealing horses from Stensen's corral, the Rio Kid shot Stensen down without mercy, while his gang of cutthroats, without which he never dares travel, turned their weapons on Ole's honest cowboys and slaughtered a number before a posse from town could reach the ranch and drive them off.

How long will the decent citizens of the Territory stand for such men as this Rio Kid in their midst? Haven't we a high enough tree to dangle him from? What's the country coming to that such a blood-stained killer dares show his face in broad daylight and cut down innocents?

Kit Carson, weakened by the difficulty he had run into in the mountains on his visit to Wolfkiller, was going back to Taos to recuperate. His chest still hurt him, painfully, although the scrapes on his cheek were healing well.

"Hannigan must be dealt with," declared Carson.

"We must be careful of Hannigan," said Don Francisco quickly.

A Mexican servant came to the door, and spoke softly to Perez. The Rio Kid, slouched in the shadows, heard what the man told the don.

"Senor Hannigan is here."

"Speak of the devil," he muttered, as he watched Don Francisco hurriedly excuse himself and leave the room.

Jed Hannigan had been in hiding, and the Rio Kid, hunting him after the fight at the basin, had had his hands full with various problems. Now Hannigan had come to the *hacienda*. The Rio Kid got up, and strolled out into the shadows of the *patio*.

Perez was near the gate. Hannigan was facing him, with light from a window falling on his face.

"I want my money, Don Francisco," Hannigan was growling. "Yuh've owed me for years and so have yore friends here. In the past month the supplies sent you fellers in Valcito run into tens of thousands of dollars for which I hold yore notes and theirs. I

mean to collect — and now — or I'll fore-
close and seize yore properties here."

"I need more time," Perez replied.

"Time?" snarled Hannigan. "Yuh've had
all yuh're goin' to get."

The great thought in the Rio Kid's mind
was that it was Hannigan who had riled up
the Navajos and been responsible for so
many deaths. Hannigan had always sent
Perez what he ordered, and never before
had demanded money. Like all his kind,
Don Francisco was not a shrewd business-
man. He had, the Rio Kid guessed, signed
whatever Hannigan put before him, too
proud and careless to argue about financial
matters. And now —

Hannigan had a legal claim to the lands
of Valcito!

"The war has cost me a great deal,"
pleaded Perez. "Much stock was run off
during the trouble, by Indians and rustlers."

"Pay," insisted Hannigan, "or I'll take your
lands and property. These mortgages and
notes are iron-clad, Perez. I'm sick of yore
high-falutin' ways with me, and now it's my
turn." Hannigan patted his breast pocket. It
rustled with papers in there.

"Good," thought the Rio Kid. "He's got
'em on him!"

Across the great *patio,* two heads were

silhouetted against a wide window. Young Art Barron sat there, with Senorita Dolores Perez at his side. The Rio Kid was aware that Barron and the girl were deeply in love. The homeless wanderer had found his place in life. He would know what to do, with his shrewd business sense and knowledge of horse markets, would Barron. He could save Perez and the fortunes of the Spanish dons in Valcito. He would marry into the family and make the great properties pay.

A few of Barron's blooded horses, including the stallion, had been recovered near the Circle S, and the mustang breed could be built up.

Hannigan was the stumbling-block. If he seized Valcito . . .

The Rio Kid was strolling over to join the party by the gate.

"Hullo, Hannigan," he said easily.

Hannigan scowled at him. "I don't want any truck with you, outlaw," he said harshly.

"Well, I got an account to settle with you, Hannigan," remarked Pryor, holding out the newspaper with the lying account of himself in it. "Eat it."

"What?"

"Eat it, I said. Yuh heard me."

"This is an outrage," Hannigan whined, but the Rio Kid's eyes frightened him.

"Start eatin'. Egghead Pete spilt the whole dirty business, how you hired him and his renegades, and the Stensen and Phillips' gangs to run that war. I didn't savvy it all till today. John Frémont supplied the answer, the key. I know what yuh're after, tryin' to ruin Perez and his friends and get their lands."

Don Francisco stared at the Rio Kid.

"What is this?" he asked.

The Rio Kid was busy with Hannigan who, afraid of the lithe scout, was chewing up pieces of his newspaper and trying to swallow it.

"No white men's court," mumbled Hannigan, blinking, "will believe Egghead Pete's lies. Everybody savvies he's a no-good, thievin' weed-chewer."

The Rio Kid nodded sadly. "I agree we couldn't convict yuh. Yore pards are all dead and can't tell on yuh, and as yuh say, Egghaid's no use to us in court. Anyway, none of 'em savvied yore game entirely. The war forced Perez deeper and deeper into yore debt. Him and his Spanish friends around Valcito signed the mortgages and notes yuh shoved under their noses."

Hannigan's face was purple as he tried to swallow mouthfuls of pulp with his lying words on it.

"However," went on Pryor, "I don't hold to all that legal stuff, Hannigan. I'll hunt yuh down when I get to it. It won't be long till I settle in full with you." He shrugged and turned his back.

Hannigan saw his chance. He swore, whipped a Colt from inside his jacket, and fired at the Rio Kid.

"He threatened me with death!" he screamed, spitting out wads of paper.

The Rio Kid, figuring Hannigan would try to finish him when he swung away, was already falling. The bullet from Hannigan's gun kissed his Stetson crown, and drove on into the house wall. Pryor, gun flashing out with the speed of legerdemain, shot back under his left armpit.

A yard from the astounded Perez, frozen where he stood, Hannigan caught the Rio Kid's lead in the nose. It pierced through to the brain, and he stood for a moment before collapsing heavily at Don Francisco's feet.

The Rio Kid jumped in, kicked away Hannigan's gun, and put a hand inside the trader's pocket. He pulled out the sheaf of papers, the mortgages and notes with which Hannigan had meant to ruin Don Perez and Valcito, by seizing the land.

Before Perez could ask what he was up to, Pryor had touched a match to the sheaf and stood there, watching them flare and burn.

At the sound of shooting, Frémont and Sherman came running out, with Kit Carson bringing up the rear, painfully leaning on O-ke-bah.

"It's all settled, gents," remarked the Rio Kid calmly. "Hannigan got what he asked for. He won't bother yuh nor will them notes, either, Perez. Frémont, I reckon now's the time to tell Don Francisco what yuh told Carson and me when we got back from the mountains."

John Frémont nodded. "I found out what Hannigan was after," Frémont announced. "The Rio Kid started me off, when he pointed out some reddish stains on the sheep wool. They were copper stains, worn off when the animals brushed against deposits in the nearby hills. While Kit and the Rio Kid were gone, I explored the neighboring ground, and there are great copper mines all about us. We decided to keep it under our hats until the proper moment."

In the morning, General Sherman prepared to take his leave of his friends at Valcito.

Bigfoot Wallace, too, was on his way.

"C'mon, Rio Kid," Bigfoot urged. "We'll haid for Santa Fé and have the biggest blow-off ever 'fore I have to get back on that tarnation stage box. I must say we didn't get much elk or grizzly huntin', dog it. What a vacation! Sleepin' near a house always did annoy me."

"I ain't goin' to Santa Fé, Bigfoot," said the Rio Kid. "Reckon I'll take a fling at Gen'ral Sherman's game in Colorado."

"Oh, shucks. Then I got to ride alone. Well, *adios*, Rio Kid — and you, too, Mexes, and all. See yuh again."

Bigfoot rode off, back to his job in Santa Fé. Kit Carson and Frémont would drop off at Taos, while the Rio Kid swung in beside General Sherman, headed for Fort Lyon. As soon as Celestino recovered from his wound, he was to follow his friend.

Sherman and the Rio Kid rode at the head of the troopers, the general's three-star guidon waving in the fresh breeze. The blue-clad, crack cavalrymen, with broad yellow stripes down the seams of their blue pants, field hats jaunty on their groomed heads, tunics spick-and-span, and gleaming high boots, made a beautiful picture. It was one that brought back with nostalgic force to Bob Pryor the days of the War, when he had been a cavalry captain and, on Saber, led his men.

But the danger trail called again, in another way, and the hot blood of the Rio Kid replied as he set Saber at a sharp clip ahead.

The employees of Thorndike Press hope you have enjoyed this Large Print book. All our Thorndike, Wheeler, and Kennebec Large Print titles are designed for easy reading, and all our books are made to last. Other Thorndike Press Large Print books are available at your library, through selected bookstores, or directly from us.

For information about titles, please call:
  (800) 223-1244

or visit our Web site at:
  http://gale.cengage.com/thorndike

To share your comments, please write:
  Publisher
  Thorndike Press
  10 Water St., Suite 310
  Waterville, ME 04901